LAST CHANCE ISLAND

OTHER NOVELS BY
NORMA CHARLES

Run Marco, Run (Ronsdale, 2011)

Chasing a Star (Ronsdale, 2009)

Bank Job (Orca, 2009, with James Heneghan)

The Girl in the Backseat (Ronsdale, 2008)

Boxcar Kid (Dundurn, 2007)

Sophie's Friend in Need (Beach Holme, 2004)

All the Way to Mexico (Raincoast, 2003)

Fuzzy Wuzzy (Coteau, 2002)

Criss Cross, Double Cross (Beach Holme, 2002)

The Accomplice (Raincoast, 2001)

Sophie, Sea to Sea (Beach Holme, 1999)

Runaway (Coteau, 1999)

Dolphin Alert! (Nelson, 1998)

Darlene's Shadow (General, 1991)

A bientôt, Croco (Scholastic, 1991)

See You Later, Alligator (Scholastic, 1991)

April Fool Heroes (Nelson, 1989)

Un poney embarrassant (Les Editions Héritage, 1989)

No Place for a Horse (General, 1988)

Amanda Grows Up (Scholastic, 1978)

Last
Chance
island

Norma Charles

RONSDALE PRESS

LAST CHANCE ISLAND
Copyright © 2016 Norma Charles

RONSDALE PRESS
3350 West 21st Avenue, Vancouver, B.C., Canada V6S 1G7
www.ronsdalepress.com

Typesetting: Julie Cochrane, in Minion 12 pt on 16
Cover Design: Julie Cochrane
Paper: Ancient Forest Friendly "Silva" (FSC) — 100% post-consumer waste,
    totally chlorine-free and acid-free

Ronsdale Press wishes to thank the following for their support of its publishing
program: the Canada Council for the Arts, the Government of Canada through the
Canada Book Fund, the British Columbia Arts Council, and the Province of British
Columbia through the British Columbia Book Publishing Tax Credit program.

Library and Archives Canada Cataloguing in Publication

Charles, Norma M., author
    Last Chance Island / Norma Charles.

Issued in print and electronic formats.
ISBN 978-1-55380-458-1 (print)
ISBN 978-1-55380-459-8 (ebook) / ISBN 978-1-55380-460-4 (pdf)

    I. Title.

PS8555.H4224L38 2016   jC813'.54   C2015-906738-3   C2015-906739-1

At Ronsdale Press we are committed to protecting the environment. To this end we
are working with Canopy and printers to phase out our use of paper produced from
ancient forests. This book is one step towards that goal.

Printed in Canada by Marquis Printing, Quebec

*for my dear friends
Sonia and Jim,
who were there at
the beginning of this story*

ACKNOWLEDGEMENTS

Thank you, Linda Bailey, Beryl Young, and James Heneghan for all your excellent suggestions with the manuscript. Thanks also to Olive John, especially for your guidance about Irish ways. And thanks to my sweetie, Brian Wood, for your continued support and advice, especially about things mechanical and nautical. Thank you, Ronald Hatch, for taking a chance on this one.

Chapter 1

KALU

MORNING HAD ARRIVED to the west coast of Africa. Another hot, dusty day. Kalu had gone to the outhouse. His teacher had suggested he go there to practise a new tune on his bamboo flute. He'd just started playing when he heard what sounded like a gun firing close by. In the school!

His first instinct was to run to help. But he stopped himself. He stashed the flute back into his belt. Then he pulled the door on the outhouse closed more snugly. And waited.

Not for long.

The kids in his class filed past the door. He held his breath. He could see them through the cracks in the wall and hear them shuffling in the dust. Some were crying. But quietly, so no one else would hear them.

Soldiers. The rebel soldiers had come for them. The march of their heavy boots was unmistakable. They had come to take the children away. The boys to become child soldiers. The girls to do unspeakable things.

There weren't many children in the school. Fewer than twenty. Kalu, who was thirteen, and his brother Oscar, fourteen, were the oldest. Oscar was taller. Their cousin Aisha was probably the youngest.

Several more shots were fired. Shouts. Terrified screams. Running. More shots. More screams.

Then the crackling of fire.

They'd set the village on fire. Soon the wind would drive the flames here. To the outhouse. To Kalu's hideout.

He eased the door open. Smoke burnt his nostrils. Already he could feel the fire's heat on his face. He saw no one.

He slipped out and crept to the schoolroom.

Empty.

Except for the teacher. He was sprawled face down on the desk, blood seeping from his head, staining the test papers he had been marking.

Kalu heard a scuffling sound and weeping. He inched to the desk and peered under. Between the teacher's knees a kid was hiding. His cousin.

"Aisha," Kalu whispered.

She scrambled out and grabbed onto Kalu's waist. She was sobbing and trembling.

"We have to get out of here." He patted her back. "The soldiers might return to be sure they got us all."

He looked out the school doorway. No soldiers. Just eye-watering smoke. Sweltering fire.

But he had to check if anyone was still in the village. Anyone alive.

"You wait in the outhouse," he whispered to Aisha. "I'll see if anyone's left."

But he couldn't even get close to the huts. Their grass roofs burst into flames with a hot whoosh, one after another. The poles he and Oscar and a couple of the uncles had erected around the village for a windbreak were burning now. No one could be left there. Not even his mother.

He shook his head. He couldn't let himself think about her. Not now. It would be better for her if she'd been shot rather than marched off by the soldiers.

"Come on, Aisha. No one's left. We have to get out of here."

Aisha had stopped sobbing, but she was still trembling. She nodded and followed him into the bush. The ground was hot under their bare feet. Kalu picked up a couple of pebbles and stashed them into his small cloth pouch along with a pinch of sweet herbs to remind him of home.

They would head to the village of their Uncle Gigi. It was a two-day walk under the blistering sun through the bush and over grassy lands where herds of sheep and goats roamed under the watchful eyes of young shepherds. But they'd have to keep off the trails in case the soldiers found them.

They arrived at dusk the next day, starving. For two days, they'd eaten nothing but a few sour berries and a bit of milk Kalu managed to coax out of a nanny goat he'd caught.

Their Uncle Gigi wasn't in the village. He'd gone to the city to try to find work. But his family gave Kalu and Aisha a bit of supper. Rice and lentils, and water to drink.

"You can sleep here tonight but you can't stay," their auntie told them. "We don't have enough food to feed even our-selves."

"Go to Sleeva," an elder said. "They always need help on the boats."

"What about Aisha?" Kalu asked his auntie. "Can Aisha stay with you?"

The auntie nodded reluctantly. "Maybe such a little thing won't eat much. And I'm sure she can work hard."

The next morning before daybreak, Kalu set off for Sleeva. They'd told him it was a small seaside town where many boats stopped to drop off cargo and pick up other goods.

Before he'd gone far, he was aware of a stealthy shadow following him. But every time he turned around, he didn't see anyone. Or anything. Was a soldier tracking him? Or a leopard?

He ducked behind a bush, fists ready, and held his breath.

A rustling of dried leaves.

Aisha! He grabbed her arm and she screamed.

When she realized it was him and had stopped screaming, he said, "You can't come, Aisha. You have to stay with Auntie."

"No." She lifted her chin defiantly. "I'm going with you. She's not my family. You are my family now."

Kalu squatted beside her. "It's going to be hard in the town. I'll have a hard enough time looking after myself. I can't look after you as well. What will you eat? Where will you sleep?"

"Like Auntie says, I don't need much to eat. And I can work. I'm strong. Look."

She held out a thin arm for him to feel her muscles.

What he saw was the determination in her eyes. He knew that she would follow him no matter what.

She was right.

They were family.

Chapter 2

SPIKE

"LILY. WAKE UP, LILY. Mother Superior wants to see you in her office."

I turned over in my narrow bed and groaned. Crap! How had the Boss-Lady figured out it was me who'd cut the wires to the annoying morning bell?

All us boarders at St. Bridgette's were so fed up with being woken up every single morning at 6:00 a.m. for prayers, we had to do something. And since I was the only one who knew how to solve the problem and had enough nerve to do it, it had been up to me.

We thought we'd all be getting one last good sleep before

spring break that was starting tomorrow. But no, here was prim Miss Jacob, the dorm supervisor, shaking my shoulder, waking me, way before dawn had even started creeping through the dorm windows.

"Come now," she whispered.

I groaned again, rubbing my eyes and pushing myself up.

"Hush," she hissed, finger to her lips. "We don't want to wake the other girls."

She handed me my dressing gown from the chair as I fumbled for slippers. She led the way out into the hallway, shutting the door to the dorm behind us with a quiet click.

As I followed her stiff back along the dimly lit hallway and down the staircase to Mother Superior's office, I racked my brains for an excuse for clipping the wire. My mind was mush.

I don't know why Miss Jacob had to accompany me. I knew the way to the office well. Over the past couple of years, I'd been summoned there often enough. Mostly about my dyed-purple hair and various piercings which were frowned upon at St. Bridgette's Catholic Boarding School for Girls.

Mother Superior was waiting for me behind her desk. But her usual stern face framed by her starched white wimple seemed almost relaxed. Maybe even a bit sympathetic? Strange.

"Thank you, Miss Jacob." She fluttered a hand. "You may go now."

Before she turned to leave, Miss Jacob gave me a pat on the

shoulder and a sort of sympathetic look as well.

A feeling of dread trickled into my insides. What was going on here?

"Please, sit down, Lily." Mother Superior's thin mouth twitched into a small and alarming smile.

Although pretty well all the girls here called me Spike (short for Spiekeford, my last name) the teachers called me Lily. I cringed whenever I heard that stupid girlie name. Sounded like I was a three-year-old wannabe princess.

But something serious was going on this morning. A lot more serious than cutting the wire to an annoying morning bell.

"My dear." Mother Superior's dark grey eyes looked right into mine. "I'm afraid I have some sad news for you." She reached over and patted my hand.

I braced myself.

"It's your father. He had a massive heart attack, and he died last night. They've just discovered his body. I'm so sorry." Her fingers were dry and cold as they curved around my hand.

I pulled in a breath and my mind swirled away. "My father? No. No. But how . . . how could he?" My voice ended in a sob.

I couldn't believe it. My father was always exercising and keeping himself active. It was true that he smoked and maybe drank too much. He wasn't that old . . .

"But, but I just talked to him last weekend and, and . . ." I crossed my arms, fingers burrowing into my armpits. Trying to keep myself together. Tears gathered and ran down my cheeks.

"My dear. We're all so terribly sorry." Mother Superior handed me a wad of tissues.

I blew my nose and tried to brush away the tears. The world whirled around me and tilted. In a single moment, everything changed. Now I had no one. No family at all. My mother had died when I was born so there'd always been just me and my father. Where would I go? Who'd look after me? A million questions clattered in my head.

After a while, Mother Superior said, "Are you all right, dear?"

I sniffed and nodded.

She gave me another gentle smile. "I was thinking that since spring break is starting tomorrow, it would be best if you packed your bag and left for home this morning. I'll have Miss Jacob help you. We'll arrange a taxi to drive you to the train station to take you home. Your father's, um, friend, Miss McPhee, will be there. She'll be making the arrangements."

My father's "um-friend" was Felicity McPhee. I called her Feefee, but not to her face. He had met her a few years ago, after which she became his live-in girlfriend and I became *persona non grata* with her. To say she and I didn't get along was putting it mildly. She couldn't stand the sight of me. And I felt exactly the same about her. In fact, she was the main reason I'd been sent off to boarding school and spent most summer holidays at various sports camps.

Somehow I got back to the dorm and pulled my duffle from the top of my closet. By then, my roomies Salina and Zoe were awake.

Salina turned on her light. "What's happening, Spike?"

I sniffed and blew my nose again.

"Boss-Lady didn't find out about the clipped wire, did she?" Zoe asked.

I shook my head. "No. It's, it's my father . . ."

"What?" Both girls rushed to my side.

"He, he just . . . died," I blubbered. "Last night . . . His heart . . ." I collapsed onto my bed and buried my face in the pillow.

Both girls hugged my back, murmuring, "Sorry, so sorry, Spike. Oh. So, so sorry . . ."

Eventually I got it together and they helped pack most of my things into my duffle, mostly dirty laundry, and I got dressed in "civvies," jeans and a sweater instead of the usual school uniform of navy tunic and long-sleeved white shirt. I left those hanging in the closet.

When Miss Jacob came to get me, I was more or less ready. After a last look around our small cluttered dorm that had been home away from home for the past few years, with goodbye hugs from Zoe and Salina, as well as from a couple of other girls who had peeked out of their dorm when they heard me leaving, I followed Miss Jacob out into the hall, dragging my stuffed duffle.

Chapter 3

KALU

AT THE SEASIDE, the air was cooler than in Kalu's village, with the breezes blowing in from the vast Atlantic Ocean. But it was smellier. Dead fish tumbled in the frothy waves at the edge of the rocky shore strewn with slimy seaweed.

Thin dogs with huge teeth and visible ribs searched the waves for edible bits of food. They growled fiercely, battling each other, coarse fur along their necks standing on end.

Kalu and Aisha didn't stay long at the beach, just long enough to walk beside it to the town. Sleeva was much bigger than their tiny village. It had rows and rows of dusty houses that ended at a long narrow wooden dock. The dock reached out into the ocean and was flanked on both sides by fishing boats attached to it by ropes. Fishermen sat under the trees at the water's edge mending nets spread out on their legs.

Kalu approached an elderly man with a beard and a kind face. "Good day, Uncle," he said. "I'm looking for work."

"You and everyone else in this town," the man grunted. "You're not from around here, are you?"

"No." Kalu couldn't tell him where he was from. The news might leak out to the soldiers that someone had escaped from the village. Someone who could tell what had happened there. How everyone had been killed or forced to join the rebel soldiers' ranks. "But I can work hard. I'm strong."

The man stared at him then motioned for him to come nearer. "I heard about a fisherman looking for help. He had two men who abandoned him. There are rumours that this fisherman is not always so honest. And he is not from around here. He's foreign. From the north. Far, far north. British, maybe. And they say that sometimes his cargo may be more than just fish. Not many would want to work for such a man."

Kalu hadn't eaten much for the three days he and Aisha had taken to walk to the coast. He was desperate.

"Which is his boat, Uncle?"

The *Irish Queen* was tied up to one of the floats. The last boat, the furthest out to sea.

A man with a white face and a blond moustache was sitting on the deck smoking a pipe, his legs stretched out.

"Excuse me, sir," Kalu said in his best school-boy English.

"I am looking for work." He had made Aisha wait up on the dock, crouched behind a barrel.

The man turned and stared at Kalu. "You don't look like much to me. Too young. Too skinny."

"I'm strong." Kalu puffed out his chest and stood his tallest. "I can work hard. Very hard. Very cheap."

But the man's attention swung to two other men, locals, who pulled up with two carts piled high with boxes and covered loosely with tarps. The boxes clinked slightly so Kalu knew they were probably filled with bottles.

The fisherman grunted at the men and pulled out his wallet, peeling off a wad of bills and giving them each a couple. Then he held the rest of the wad in front of them. "This is yours when the boxes have all been safely stowed below in the hold . . ."

"But you pay for boxes now," one of the men said, holding out his hand.

"No way," the fisherman said. "You want money? You get it when all the boxes are on my boat." He crossed his arms and stood tall, staring down at them.

The men shrugged at each other and started unloading the boxes onto the boat and carrying them down into the boat's hold. But they didn't look happy. Especially when the man tried to hurry them.

"Come on. We haven't got all day." He glanced up at the dock as if he was expecting someone to rush down any minute and apprehend him.

Kalu saw his chance. He grabbed a box and sprinted onto

the boat, carrying it down the ladder into the hold, a deep tank-sort of space with no windows. It was even smellier down here than on the beach. Rotten dead fish. Kalu tried not to inhale as he pushed the box into a corner and rushed back up to grab another box. And another.

When the fisherman turned away to go into a cabin at the front of the boat, Kalu waved to Aisha. She ran down the ramp to join him, her bare feet flying over the boards.

Kalu told her to hurry down into the hold before the fisherman saw her and to help push the boxes into piles.

With the two men helping, soon the boxes in the carts were gone.

And so was the fisherman. He'd started the engine in the cabin. Kalu was coming up the ladder from the hold when he saw the fisherman had already pulled in his ropes and his boat was drifting away from the dock.

The two men who'd delivered the boxes were left on the float with their empty carts. They were shouting angrily at the fisherman, shaking their fists at him.

As far as Kalu could make out, the fisherman had left without paying them the rest of what he owed.

Soon the boat had left the dock and the town behind and they were far out to sea.

The fisherman was in high spirits. He shouted to Kalu from inside the cabin where he was steering the boat. "Crack open one of those boxes, boy, and bring me up a bottle. We got to celebrate."

Kalu climbed back down into the hold. Aisha was still there, crouched beside the piles of boxes. "He wants a bottle from one of these boxes."

She helped him open one but it didn't have any bottles. It was full of something packed in plastic bags. Kalu had no idea what it was. He opened another box. That one contained bottles. He pulled out one. "Finest Jamaican Rum," he read the label. "So many boxes. So many bottles. Must be worth a fortune. No wonder those men were so angry. He probably owed them for all this rum and whatever's in those plastic bags."

The fisherman opened the bottle with his teeth and took a long drink. "Ah! Now if that don't settle the nerves and soothe the soul, I don't know what will." He grinned.

Kalu held onto the swaying deck and stared back at where they'd come from. Now the land was just a smudge on the horizon and they were surrounded by the heaving blue-green ocean. Where they were heading, he had no idea. But it had to be better than back there on land where it was just a matter of time before the soldiers found him and Aisha.

He patted his pocket. All he had was his small cloth bag with the pebbles from home and the sweet herbs. And his bamboo flute tucked into his belt.

Chapter 4

SPIKE

THE TAXI AND TRAIN ride back home were uneventful, as usual. I didn't expect Feefee to meet me at the train station, and she didn't. My father's lawyer, Farley Wilson, was there instead.

"Sorry for your loss," he mumbled as he led the way to the underground car park. His pale hair was thinner than the last time I'd seen him, and his belly had definitely expanded. If anyone was going to die of a heart attack, it should have been him. He got puffed out even going *down* stairs.

I followed him, bouncing my duffle down the cement steps. We stopped beside a sleek black Jaguar. My father's pride and joy. I was planning to ask him to teach me how to drive it during spring break. And there was old Farley, already helping himself to it. Another stab to my heart.

He beeped the trunk open but didn't offer to lift my duffle into it, so I levered it up myself and sat in the front passenger seat, leaning back into its smooth and comforting leather. I caught a faint whiff of my father, a combo of his aftershave and those after-dinner cigars he savoured. It was hard to stop tears from trickling down my cheeks.

When we got home, I dragged my duffle down the hallway. Feefee was in my father's study, sitting behind his desk, rummaging through his drawers.

"Oh, there you are. You're back," she said, staring in my direction. No smile of welcome or sympathy there.

I ran my fingers through my long purple bangs and stared back.

Did she have to make it so obvious she hated my guts?

"Funeral the day after tomorrow. No use waiting around for it. He wouldn't have liked that."

What a cold witch, I thought. I turned away to go up to my room.

"But what to do with you ... That's the problem." She tapped the top of the desk with her long red fingernails, probably scratching its pristine varnished surface.

"What do you mean?"

"No point you hanging around here after the funeral, now is there?" She picked up a nail file and stroked the nail on her ring finger, the one where a hefty diamond ring glittered. "We'll have to find you a nice home where you'll belong. So

I've been doing a lot of searching, trying to track down your next of kin. And I've located someone that might work. An aunt, sort of. A Maureen Calhoun. Lives in Ireland. Her name and number are in your father's address book here. I was about to put in a call to her." And she lifted the receiver and began dialling.

Maureen Calhoun? The name was vaguely familiar. My father had mentioned her occasionally, and there'd been the odd Christmas card over the years, but she and my father certainly weren't close. She was my mother's sister. Or cousin, maybe? Personally, I wouldn't know her from a stranger in the street.

"Maureen Calhoun?" Feefee said into the receiver with the fake English accent she often used on the phone. She pressed a button so it was on speakerphone.

"Yes?" A woman's voice came through the static.

"This is Felicity McPhee from Ontario."

"Felicity McPhee?"

"We've never met. I'm afraid I have some bad news. It's about John Spiekeford. He just died. Last night."

"Lela's husband? Oh, I am sorry to hear that. So sorry." I didn't recognize the voice. A soft Irish accent.

"Yes. A heart attack. Sudden, like. The thing is, there's John's daughter, Lily. She's fifteen, too young to live on her own. Now, you're the next of kin."

"I am? Really?"

"Yes. John didn't have any other family to speak of. I mean, there's an old uncle in Winnipeg, but no one suitable."

"Suitable?"

"Yes. To take the child, you see. I mean, she certainly can't stay here."

"But I live on an island, alone. I'm the lighthouse keeper here on Last Chance. This is no place for a child."

Not exactly your most friendly welcome. Well, that was fine with me. I didn't want to go there anyway. Who in their right mind would want to live on some god-forsaken island a million miles from civilization?

But Feefee persisted. "Lily could be a help for you around the place. She's a big strong girl."

That was another bone of contention between us. I was your regular-sized fifteen-year-old and she was always trying to put me on some fad diet so I could become as skinny and scrawny as she was.

"Anyways, at the moment, with John gone, there simply is no one else to take her."

"But she must still be in school? There's no school here or any other children."

"Oh, I'm sure she'd love to do some kind of online course. How about she stay with you just until we have something else figured out? Maybe that uncle in Winnipeg could take her. Once I manage to track him down."

I was feeling more and more like a piece of dirty old baggage no one wanted.

"Well . . . I guess we could try it." Still not much enthusiasm there. "For a while, maybe. How would she get here?"

"I'll send her over with John's lawyer, Farley Wilson. It's

the least he can do for what we've been paying him. I'll let you know when to expect her. Probably soon. Like early next week."

I didn't wait to hear the rest of the conversation. I lugged my duffle up the carpeted stairs to my room.

My whole life was a mess. No father. No home. No family. No one.

And here I was being shipped off to God-knows-where. I knew I didn't have any choice.

My father and Feefee had been living in this house for a couple of years now. I did have a bedroom where I could stay on school holidays, but it never felt much like home. It had always been *her* house, with *her* choice of stuff all around.

Now I had nothing. Maybe there'd eventually be some kind of inheritance from my father's estate. Probably not much after she dug her greedy hands into it.

Still, once I arrived at wherever that island was, there'd be nothing stopping me from leaving and heading out on my own. Make my own life. That was one good thing ... It wasn't like I was being sent to Alcatraz.

Right?

Chapter 5

KALU

KALU STARED OUT at the heaving ocean. They were so far out now that he'd lost sight of land.

"So what's your name, boy?" the fisherman raised his cap and asked.

"Kalu."

"Ever worked on a boat before?"

Kalu shook his head.

"Well, Kalu. This is going to be a mighty fine learning experience for you. How about starting by rustling us up some grub?"

"Grub?"

"Food. You know. Something to eat. You sure look like you could do with a good meal or two. I can almost see through you, you're so thin."

"Where is food?" Kalu looked around the deck.

"It's below. In the galley."

Kalu turned to head back down the hold. He sure hoped there was something other than rotten fish to eat.

"Not there, kid. The galley." The man pointed to a door beside the cabin.

When Kalu opened the door he saw steep steps that led down to another area. It was a narrow room lined on one side with cupboards and a gas stove. And on the other, three narrow bunks built into the side of the boat. They were a lot like the beds built into the side of his stick-and-mud house back home, one for his brother and him, and the other for his mother . . .

No. He couldn't think about that now.

After the bright sunshine that bounced off the waves up on the deck, it was quite dark down here in what the fisherman called the galley. The only light was the sunshine filtering in the entrance. There were curtains over a couple of glass windows on both sides. He pulled the curtains aside so he could get a better look around. The first cupboard he peered into was filled with cups and plates and bowls. No food that he could see.

The next cupboard held only cans with pictures of food on them. He pulled one out with a picture of some beans and sniffed it. Sure didn't smell like food. Anyway, if the can did hold food, how did you get it out? He turned the can over. There wasn't an opening anywhere that he could see.

He opened another cupboard lower down and found big glass jars filled with rice and flour and sugar, even dried beans and lentils. Now that was better. He eased out the rice jar and wished he'd paid more attention when his mother cooked rice. How did she do it? He knew he'd need some water. But how much?

He unscrewed the lid. There was a sort of scoop inside. He scooped out two helpings into a pot, then looked around for water. The swaying of the curtains caught his eye. He stared out the small window. Water. Right. The boat was surrounded by water. He got a bowl and climbed back up on deck. He'd just lower the bowl into the water and get some. One bowlful should be enough.

"Hey, boy," the fisherman called to him as he leaned over the railing to scoop up the water. "What you trying to do? Drown yourself?"

"I get water. To cook rice."

The fisherman smacked his knee and laughed and laughed. "That's a good one, kid. We don't use sea water for cooking rice, or anything. Just for washing up the dishes and swabbing the deck. That's about it."

"Oh." Kalu stood there. "Um. Where is water for the cooking?"

"Right. Looks like I'll have to show you around. I'll just

put the boat on automatic pilot here. The waves are calm enough at the moment. We have to close up the hold anyways."

Close the hold? Oh no! What about Aisha?

Chapter 6

SPIKE

MY FATHER'S FUNERAL a couple of days later was a low-key affair, to say the least. A few friends from his office came to the church for a requiem mass along with a number of little old ladies who attend mass every morning, but no one came back to our house after. I went straight up to my bedroom and started packing for the trip to Ireland the next day. No point hanging around where I wasn't wanted.

One thing about Feefee, she sure could get things done fast when she wanted to. And getting rid of me was top on her list of priorities.

I dumped the stuff out of my duffle. Most of it was dirty

laundry, but the clean jeans, t-shirts and sweaters I packed into a wheeled suitcase and added a couple of my favourite books. One was a *Popular Mechanics* manual about motors. I loved studying the illustrations that showed how the gears and pistons and different parts all fitted together like a complex puzzle. Cool.

I wished I could be returning to St. Bridgette's after spring break so I could be back with my friends, but that just wasn't going to happen. A summer camp would have been nice too, but it wasn't summer yet.

The best thing about last summer's camp on Saltery Island was the boats. I tried to learn everything there was to learn about every kind of boat from motorboats to rowboats and kayaks. It was the motorboats I loved the most. When you turned the motor on high and the boat was skidding across the water, you got an amazing sense of power.

I gazed around the bedroom. Pale pink walls, stupid flowery ruffles on the bed and a little-girl princess desk I never used. All designed by guess-who. Sucking up to my father. Perfect for his sweet daughter called "Lily" . . .

Sure wouldn't be missing this baby room.

Thick bushes grew right up against the house. Even on the sunniest days, the room was so dim you had to turn on the lights to read. The windows were sealed shut so I couldn't open them to let out the stuffiness.

I remembered whole weekends when I'd be cooped up here, waiting for time alone with my father. I hate to admit it but the truth is, sometimes he didn't seem all that enthusiastic about spending time with me. Especially after Feefee came along.

Tears stung my eyes, and I brushed them away angrily. I hated when that happened. Not only was I missing my father, but now I was totally alone.

I kicked a couple of cushions onto the floor, blew my nose and finished packing.

I was about to zip up the suitcase when I remembered my silver watch. Sure couldn't leave that behind. It was the only thing I had of my mother's. I searched through my duffle for it. There it was in the top flap.

The watch fitted snugly into a leather pouch with a beaded string I wore around my neck a lot of the time. A sort of symbol had been worked into the leather. Three spiral circles connected by a triangle in the centre. I had often wondered if the symbol meant anything. Or was it just a decoration?

The watch was old, so old it didn't have a battery, so if I forgot to wind it, it stopped working. I lifted it to my ear and listened. Its tick was sort of like a gentle rain falling on a metal rooftop. Cool to think I could hear the very same sound my own mother once heard.

I pulled the string over my head, cupping the pouch in my palm and breathed in the sweet leather smell. The past few years, the watch had become a talisman. As long as I had it I knew I'd be OK. No matter what.

I dug out my earphones and turned on my iPod. Zolda's

voice chanted the song with no real words, only a pulsing melody. I shut my eyes and started swaying to the beat. If I danced hard enough, and the beat was loud enough, maybe it would drown the pain, the loneliness, the fear.

Music washed over me, urging my feet and hands to move until I was dancing like a wild thing around the space at the foot of the bed.

Chapter 7

KALU

WHEN THE FISHERMAN left the cabin to join Kalu, he said, "You want to grab the other side of the lid there and we'll just slide it into place over the hold. Keep our precious cargo down there all nice and dry."

"Ah, Mister," Kalu hesitated. The fisherman was going to find out about Aisha sooner or later, so it may as well be now. "Aisha," he shouted down into the hold. "Come up now."

The fisherman looked at him as if he was crazy. When Aisha's head popped out of the hold, he looked so shocked Kalu thought he would have tumbled overboard if he hadn't grabbed the railing.

"Where — where did she come from?" His pale eyes were huge in his pale face.

"Um," Kalu stammered. "This is Aisha. She is my cousin."

"Your cousin?" The fisherman peered down into the hold. "Are there any more of you hiding down there?"

"No, no. Just my cousin. She knows cooking. She is very good cooking. She always helps the aunties make dinner."

The fisherman stared from Kalu to Aisha. And back to Kalu. Then he laughed. "Right-o, then. Two of you for the price of one."

Kalu nodded.

The fisherman laughed again and took Kalu up to the wheelhouse to show him how to steer the boat and keep his eyes open for any debris on the water they'd have to avoid.

"Though there shouldn't be much out here so far from land," he told him. "And try to keep the boat hitting the waves at a bit of an angle, like this. Good. You've got it. I'll just go and show our Miss Aisha around the galley."

The next few days slipped by as Kalu learnt more about steering the boat, heading northwest, then after a few days, straight north. As the air grew cooler, Mister Elliot, which was the fisherman's name, gave Kalu a green woolly hat.

"Rule of the sea, kid. If your head's warm, the rest of you will be too."

He showed Kalu how to lower the fishing nets into the sea and raise them again, squirming with silver-coloured bits of sunshine that were the fish.

Before stashing them into the gigantic refrigerated fish bins down in the hold, he'd grab a couple of big ones. "These will do fine for our supper. What do you say now, Kalu? Think our Miss Aisha will be able to cook them?"

Mister Elliot showed her how to work the gas burner and she learnt fast. He even showed her how to open those cans with the pictures of beans or corn or tomatoes on them with what he called a can opener. Kalu thought it was magic.

"Your fish and rice dish is pretty darn good, Miss Aisha," Mister Elliot said, grinning at her one evening.

She smiled back at him, showing a space in her mouth where a front tooth had fallen out that day.

Kalu wondered how long this boat trip was going to last. Where was Mister Elliot heading? What would happen to him and Aisha once they got there?

Each evening when the sun was low on the horizon, Kalu pulled out his bamboo flute. It was a link to his village, to his family. As the orange ball sank into the vast heaving ocean, Kalu played his flute. He played the tunes he remembered from when he was small, and all the people in the village had gathered around a fire in the evening to laugh and talk about the day, and to sing the sun to sleep for the night. While he played his flute, he remembered his family, his cousins, his brother.

Most of all, he remembered his mother and her kind smile and gentle touch.

He played the sweet melodies until the sun had gone, and its golden rays had faded into the purple evening sky.

His heart dipped with sadness when he thought he would never see his mother's face again.

Chapter 8

SPIKE

A FEW DAYS LATER, after an excruciating seven-hour flight across the Atlantic, it was sunset when Farley and I finally landed at the Dublin airport. Because there was no train until the next morning to the other side of Ireland, where my aunt lived on Last Chance Island, we had to check into a hotel for the night.

To get downtown, we took a taxi through crazy rush-hour traffic where everyone was driving on the wrong side of the road. We finally pulled to a stop in front of the Dublin Arms Hotel. It looked as if it'd been built before the Crusades. Worn rugs carpeted the lobby and two old armchairs sagged beside a table with a plastic vase of artificial flowers. All even more suffocating and stuffy than the plane.

I pulled out a tissue and blew my nose, careful, as usual. I didn't want to dislodge my nose ring. The hotel clerk was taking forever to check us in. I couldn't stand another stifling minute. I'd burst if I didn't get out of there.

"I'm taking a look around town," I told Farley.

"I don't think so, Lily . . ."

I narrowed my eyes and gave him a double-whammy stare. Then I headed for the door, leaving my luggage for him to deal with.

"Listen . . ." He started after me.

I skipped down the hotel steps and escaped, joining the crowd on the busy sidewalk. I glanced back. He hadn't followed me so I pushed my hands deep into my jeans pockets and slouched along, sucking in the evening air loaded with car exhaust and cooking smells. But at least it was cooler out here.

By then it was dark out except for pools of light under old-fashioned streetlights. Bumper-to-bumper traffic wound along the narrow street between old greystone buildings.

A couple of blocks away, I heard strains of wild street music wafting from a cluster of musicians. I saw they were on some steps under a streetlight in front of a crowd. Red and purple scarves floated around a bunch of kids dancing, hypnotized by the music.

A fiddler with a mass of curly hair bounced up and down

in time to the beat beside a woman playing a flute. Behind them, strumming the rhythm, was a bass player wearing a crazy orange top hat that had toppled sideways. A dude with long black hair was thumping a tambourine and weaving his shoulders, flashing a white-toothed smile, encouraging the dancers.

The music lured me in too. I joined the dancers and whirled along with them, throwing up my hands, clapping, and leaping about.

Then he started . . . The dude with long black hair shut his eyes and sang in such a hauntingly high voice it sent shivers up the back of my neck. I couldn't make out the words but his song was filled with deep longing and I was drawn to him, spellbound. Like iron filings to a magnet. It made me dance, swaying back and forth, then whirling, twirling, kicking, looping. The song went on and on. Mesmerizing. No other word for it.

Eventually the song came to an end, but the band immediately started up another, as wonderful as the first. I threw myself into the dance even more, circling a couple of girls dressed in flowing skirts. I mirrored their movements and extended them. Grinning, they mirrored mine. The music grew louder and faster, and we danced faster and wilder. Then the music lurched to an abrupt end.

Breathing hard, I joined everyone clapping, stomping my feet and hooting, calling out, begging for more, more!

But the singer raised his arm. "Are ye not allowing us a wee break? Sure now, we're all fittin' to being exhausted."

So we stopped begging, and the other musicians put down their instruments and wiped their faces on their shirtsleeves. But the singer beckoned to me with a smile.

"Come now, love. Where'd you learn to dance like that?"

I was still trying to catch my breath so I shrugged and smiled back at him. I was wearing the leather pouch with my mother's watch around my neck and it had come out of my shirt.

He reached down and cupped the pouch, noticing the three-swirl decoration on it.

"Ah, the triskelion. Of course." Nodding, he stared into my eyes. His were a startling clear blue. I'd never seen eyes such an intense blue. "I knew you must be one of us, a kindred spirit, a traveller. Come now, meet our Savannah and Jake."

Traveller? What's he talking about?

Turning to the other band members, he grinned down at me. "Tell me now. Isn't she a beaut?"

The flute player whose name was Savannah grinned at me as well. "Love the purple hair. Might be exactly what we're looking for, Kieran. Another dancer for our troupe." Savannah seemed older than the rest of the kids. Plump and comfortable in a long multi-coloured kaftan. She was wearing a silver medallion around her neck with the same design as on my pouch. What had the tall singer called it? A triskelion.

The bass player nodded. "Come have a drink with us, darlin', so we can talk."

The other musicians welcomed me like a long-lost cousin. Funny. Someone pushed a bottle of water into my hands. Someone else offered me a pastry from a bakery box. Smiling faces surrounded me. I'd never felt so welcomed.

"I'm Kieran, and now what's your name, love?" Mr. Blue-eyes asked.

"Uh, Spike," I said, sipping the water.

"Spike. Ooo, I like it. Where have you come from?"

"Ah . . ." I hesitated. Should I be trusting these strangers? But his smile was so friendly. "Canada," I told him. "Just flew in."

"Canada. Exotic." He raised his eyebrows. Not only did he have the bluest eyes I'd ever seen, they were fringed with thick black lashes. "Now, Spike. You must come travellin' with us. We're leavin' in the morning for Belfast where we have a gig at the Metro on Saturday."

"Belfast?"

He nodded. "And like Savannah says, we're needing a couple more dancers to pull in the crowds, like. You're perfect." He stroked my bristly hair lightly, tugging the purple bangs. "Cute."

But I shook my head. After all, I didn't know anything about him. Or his group. "I really don't know . . ."

"If you can't join us now, we'll be back here in Dublin next week, so we will. Back to our squat down by the canal." He was still grinning at me.

Couldn't help it. I found myself grinning like a freak back

at him. I'd so love to join this bunch of musicians. They were so nice. So friendly. But I hardly knew them. I shook my head.

"But you must. You absolutely must. Where else do you have to be?"

"Lily! There you are!"

Crap! It was old Farley! I cringed when I heard his voice calling me over the mob of fans. My father's stupid lawyer had tracked me down.

I tried to duck behind Kieran but the lawyer pushed through the crowd until he could reach me. His hand closed over my arm, fingers digging in just above my elbow.

"I've been searching all over for you, Lily," he hissed in my ear, tugging me down the steps. "What are you doing here anyway? You know we have to get up early for the train in the morning. Come on. We're going back to the hotel."

"Let me go, you ..." I spat out at him, jerking my arm away. "You're not the boss of me ..."

He sucked in a breath, face growing redder with rage. "Now you listen to me, young lady ..."

"So, is this gentleman bothering you now, Spike?" Kieran stooped down to ask me.

"See here, young man ..." the lawyer blustered.

"No. No, I'm OK. Really." This was all so embarrassing. "But I have to go now. We're leaving early in the morning."

He gazed down at me, actually looking disappointed. "Look, Spike. When you're back in town, come on over to the squat. Just down by the canal at the bottom of Connolly Road. Ask anyone for me. Kieran O'Grady. It's a greystone house. You can't miss it. Bigger than it looks so there's plenty of room."

I stared up into his intense blues. "I'll come when I can," I promised.

Then I trudged after Farley, back to the suffocating hotel, back to my friggin' suffocating life.

Oh, what I'd give to stay with the musicians. And they wanted me. They actually liked me. And recognized me as a kindred spirit. What did they call themselves? Travellers. Yes. That's what I wanted to be. A traveller, travelling around the country, living here and there, making music, singing and dancing. Like in one of my favourite books, *Traveller's Dance*. About a boy who did just that. He joined a troupe that travelled all over the country making music.

A plan began to hatch in my head. First thing I'll do when I finally shake old Farley, is escape and hop the train back to Dublin and join these travellers. Down by the canal at the bottom of Connolly Road, Kieran O'Grady said. Tall gorgeous Kieran O'Grady. Shouldn't be hard to find.

The whole thing sounded like a dream. An incredible dream.

What did I have to lose?

Chapter 9

KALU

ONE DAY, A FEW WEEKS later, Kalu was swabbing the deck of the *Irish Queen*, mopping it with a bucket of soapy seawater. Mister Elliot was sitting in the cabin at the wheel listening to the shortwave radio as he often did. Kalu noticed the more the man listened, the deeper the frown on his forehead became.

Something was wrong. Kalu soon found out what.

"Hey, Kalu. Come here a minute," the fisherman called.

Mop in hand, Kalu stood at the door.

"Bad news, kid. Very bad news. The Irish coast guard is out checking every boat in these waters for illegal migrants. A bunch has just been spotted in fishing boats off the coast of Portugal and coast guard think they may be heading this way."

"Illegal migrants?" Those were English words Kalu didn't know.

"It's people who are trying to escape from their country and go to another one without permission."

"Oh." That was what he and Aisha were. "Illegal migrants."

"What will happen if they find us?"

"Don't know. Probably throw the whole lot of us into some horrible stinking jail. Maybe ship you and your cousin to God-knows-where. Also, I don't think they'll approve of my, um, liquid cargo. Or the other stuff we've got stashed down there in the hold."

Mister Elliot pulled out a rolled chart from his chart case and spread it onto the table. "Let's see. Here's a detailed chart of the southwest coast of our sweet green Ireland." He squinted at his chart and pointed. "Looks like our closest land would be this island."

To Kalu, the chart looked like a whole lot of blue sprinkled with a few squiggles of colour and edged by a strip of green. If it were a picture of what was around them now, that would be right. They'd seen nothing but the boundless blue ocean since they left Sleeva a couple of weeks ago, except for several brief stops for fuel and fresh water at quiet coastal villages along the way. Mister Elliot said he wanted to get home to Ireland as fast as he could, to unload his cargo.

"First island we'll come to," he said. "Looks like our best bet."

"Best bet?" Kalu didn't know what he was talking about.

"Look, Kalu. Here's what we'll do. When we get close to this island, I'll row you and Miss Aisha in with some water and some grub. You stay there a couple days. And when I get the all clear, that the coast guard has left the area, I'll come back and pick you up. How does that sound?"

Kalu shrugged. He knew he had no choice.

The island came in sight quite soon after. At first it was a speck of green and mist in the vast surging ocean of blue. As the boat motored closer, Kalu saw that the island looked as if it was made up of steep-sided rocky cliffs with a few bushes, ferns and spindly trees.

"Looks like a small beach just in here." Mister Elliot looked out and then pointed at the chart. As the boat drew nearer, he dropped the anchor, reversed and set it. Then he switched off the engine. "OK, kid. Grab some supplies. Couple of water bottles. Some sardines. Crackers, cheese. Look. We got to hurry, OK? They might already be onto us. The coast guard. They could be here any minute."

He untied the inflated lifeboat that was attached to the deck and lowered it into the water with a splash while Kalu and Aisha loaded up a plastic shopping bag with food and water from the galley. Kalu made sure he had his small pouch from home in his pocket and his bamboo flute.

"Come on, kids." Mister Elliot's voice crackled with tension. "We got to push off. Now."

The small lifeboat bobbed in the waves at the side of the fishing boat. Aisha hesitated. She was really scared to get into it.

Kalu was scared, too, but he couldn't let on. "It's OK," he whispered to her in their language. "We don't have far to go. We have to do this, Aisha. We have to hurry."

He climbed in first and helped her down into the bouncy boat. She cowered beside him, gripping the wooden seat that stretched across the little dinghy. He could feel her trembling with fear so he smiled his bravest smile and patted her knee.

Mister Elliot started up the motor in the little boat and soon they were on their way bashing through the waves to the island.

"Couple days," Mister Elliot told them, as they stepped over the gunnels into the cold shallow water and waded onto a rocky beach with their bag of food. "Couple days and I'll be back for you two."

As the little dinghy headed back to the boat, Kalu raised his hand goodbye and wondered if they'd ever see him again.

Chapter 10

SPIKE

THE NEXT DAY WE SPENT most of it on a long boring train ride from the Dublin station, travelling right across the whole of Ireland through mostly rolling green hills and blink-and-it's-gone villages.

Farley Wilson was still grumpy from last night. He nattered at me about proper respect toward elders and behaving properly at my aunt's place. I mostly ignored him, just stared out the train window, trying to memorize the route. After I managed my escape, I'd be repeating this trip. As soon as I got rid of this "police escort" Feefee had sent along to make sure I got to Last Chance Island in one piece, I was hitting the road back to Dublin and meeting up with Kieran and his gang.

After the early train, there was a long boring taxi ride through more rolling green hills and finally we reached the Blue Star Wharf, at the edge of a village with the weird sounding name of Skibberoo. Although it wasn't even noon yet, it felt like it had taken us practically the entire day to get here.

I was wrecked. Could barely keep my eyes open.

The wharf was deserted except for an elderly dude tinkering away on something. A broken-down boat engine, maybe? As Farley approached him, I stared at a row of dilapidated boats bouncing against the dock. One had *Seamus Water Taxi* painted on its side in peeling letters.

"Swanky," I muttered, plopping down on my suitcase and pulling the gum out of my mouth in a long pink string.

"Excuse me, sir," the lawyer said to the elderly man in a loud voice as though he thought the man was deaf. "Do you know anyone who could take this young lady out to Maureen Calhoun's? She's at the lighthouse on Last Chance Island."

The elderly man turned slowly and stared with piercing black eyes. Right at me. For a minute, he didn't say anything. Like he hadn't heard.

"Maureen Calhoun. Last Chance Island?" the lawyer repeated, even louder. "You know her?"

"Ah," the old dude said so quietly I had to strain to hear. "She's come, so she has."

"What d'you say?" the lawyer asked.

"I'll take the girl to Maureen Calhoun. I'll take her now."

"Good. Thanks." The lawyer gave him some money. Then while saying goodbye, he issued a predictable warning again, telling me that staying with Maureen Calhoun and behaving in a civilized manner was my last chance. "If it doesn't work out on the island, it'll probably be foster care for you." He looked stern, and wagged his finger at me. "So I'd watch my manners if I were you."

Blah, blah, blah. As if I hadn't heard it all before. "How can anyone be so bloody boring?" I muttered under my breath. Turning my back on him, I followed the old man down a short wooden ramp, bouncing my suitcase to the boat with *Seamus Water Taxi* on its side. I heaved the suitcase over the boat's gunnels and climbed in after it. Taking a deep breath I looked around for a place to sit.

"Here." The old man pointed to a vinyl cushion on a wooden seat that stretched across the deck under a sort of roof but the sides were open. He gave me a faded orange life preserver and nodded to me to put it on.

"This one's seen better days," I muttered, pushing my hands through the armholes and cinching it around my waist. My nose wrinkled at its musty smell, and I stared out to sea.

Exactly where were we heading? I couldn't see any sign of an island out there, just a blank misty skyline. A bunch of sea birds circled overhead, pointed wings outstretched, squawking and whistling. They looked so free. They could come and go wherever and whenever they pleased.

The old man started the motor. A 60-horsepower Yamaha. Not as big or powerful as the motor on the boat my father used to keep for cruising around the lake. But this motor sounded well-tuned and oiled. The man shifted it into gear and the boat left the dock, buzzing out into the open water.

I kept my back to Farley on the wharf so if he was waving goodbye, I didn't know. Or care.

The old man stood at the bow of the boat steering. When we left the protected bay, waves hit the boat's hull and it lurched and rocked, but he balanced easily. Although stooped, he was tall with a long weather-creased face, hooked nose, and a thick gold earring in one ear. He was wearing a tattered seaman's hat with a worn brim.

In fact, he looked as if he could be a retired pirate or something. Maybe he was still a pirate and had just captured me and would be holding me for ransom. Ransom, Feefee would certainly never pay. She'd be so glad to get rid of me. I could imagine her saying, "Good riddance to bad rubbish."

I gulped and stared around. If it turned out that he was a pirate, I couldn't think how I'd escape. I'd just have to hang on and see what happens.

As the boat turned into open water, a stiff wind blew spray into my face and it started raining. Heavy drops plopped into the sea. I brushed the spray away with my sleeve and hunkered down into my coat. I forced myself to think about something positive. OK, those musicians I met last night in Dublin. I hummed one of their tunes as I pictured them playing and singing. Oh, how I wished I was with them. Won't be long before I could get away, I told myself. Won't be long . . .

An especially big wave smacked the boat. Sea water drenched my hair and my bangs ended up plastered over my eyes. "Man, this place sucks." I pushed the bangs from my face. Licking salty lips and shivering, I stared back at the bleak rocky headland we were leaving. "This has got to be nowhere, man. No where."

But my heart was pounding. I was worried. This boat could be heading anywhere. A pirate's hideout. Or even over the edge of the earth.

"Stupid," I told myself. "Don't be so stupid. 'Course, it's not." I felt around my neck for my mother's watch. It wasn't there. Then I remembered I'd packed it away in my suitcase that morning. I couldn't chance losing it. Wish I had it right here though. I stared down at my suitcase. Too much trouble to fish it out now.

Seamus glanced back at me, his eyes black and intense. "You're Lela's girl." He raised his voice above the motor's drone. "I knew you at once."

My stomach did a flip. "My mother? You knew my mother?"

"I knew her well." He nodded, his eyes turned to the waves now.

"Really? How well did you know her?"

"We were close. Like kin."

"Oh! What was she like?"

"Brave," Seamus said.

I waited for more but now the old man was silent, watching the distant horizon.

"That's it? Brave?" I huffed. "That's all you can tell me about her?"

Seamus just tugged the worn brim of his hat lower and didn't offer any more information.

We were far from the shore now, in deep water and heavy waves, heading for the horizon. There was a smudge in the mist. Must be the island. Last Chance Island.

Chapter 11

KALU

NO SOONER HAD the *Irish Queen* pulled out of sight when it started to rain. Not the sweet gentle rain Kalu was used to. The rain that nourished the African soil so their village gardens would grow their yams and melons. The rain on this island was heavy and cold. So cold it seemed to seep right into his bones. He pulled his woolly hat down lower over his ears.

Aisha crouched on the rocks under a bush at the water's edge, shivering, struggling to tug her wet shirt and a ragged shawl around her back for warmth. Kalu searched the beach for shelter, somewhere they could hunker down out of the rain.

"Come closer to the cliff, Aisha. It's not so wet here." He spoke to her in their own language. So much easier than always struggling to find the right English words to use as he had to with Mister Elliot.

She followed him away from the water to some rocks beside a high mossy cliff. He dumped their food out behind a rock and fashioned a sort of cape for her out of the plastic bag.

"This will keep the rain off your back at least," he said as he adjusted it around her shoulders.

She nodded and blinked up at him, trying to smile through her shivers.

"How about a bit to eat?" he said. "That will make us feel better."

It was too wet to try to start a fire. Besides, he had only a few matches in his denim bag. He would keep those for later when it was dark and they'd really need a fire. Maybe by then the rain would have stopped.

He sat on a rock beside Aisha and they shared a lump of cheese and munched on some hard crackers, which was difficult for Aisha without her two front teeth. Already their breakfast of porridge and milk from a can along with the strong hot tea a few hours ago in the dry and cozy galley on the boat felt like another life.

"Won't be long and Mister Elliot will be back for us." Kalu tried to cheer up his cousin.

She nodded and shivered some more.

He pulled out his flute and played some lively tunes to chase away the gloom, but the wind shifted and the driving rain found them.

"Look. You stay here with the food and I'll go look for a better shelter for us." He tucked his flute back into his belt.

"Yes." She pulled the plastic cape closer around her back.

There seemed to be a sort of faint path that ran along the bottom of the cliff. Maybe it had been made by animals? Kalu looked around, checking for creatures lurking in the shadows. He knew from his studies in geography at school that lions and leopards and hyenas didn't live in northern countries, but other wild animals did. Dangerous animals like bears and wolves. Was it these animals that had made this path, he wondered, as he followed it along the bottom of the cliff. Then the path disappeared. It came to a place where the cliff jutted out toward the sea and just disappeared.

Now if he were an animal and he came to such a cliff, where would he go? He probably wouldn't follow it out over the rocks toward the water. He wouldn't want to get wet. He was about to return to Aisha and search for shelter on the other side of her. But a slight shadow in the mossy cliff caught his eye. Could the path go up this cliff at a sort of diagonal?

He followed it, climbing the steep cliff, his bare toes digging into the slippery moss. The path took him up the cliff, up to a ledge so narrow, there was barely enough room for his feet. Leaning against the cliff, he edged himself along until the ledge widened a little so he could stand with two feet together.

Then it widened even more as it came to a thick bush growing right out of a crack in the rock. The bush blocked his progress, so he pushed at it to see if there was a way past. To his surprise, behind the bush was a hollow in the rock. He squatted down to check it out and found it wasn't just a hollow. It was a sort of cave, a shallow cave. He felt the ground inside and found it was dry and out of the rain.

"I found it!" he shouted down to Aisha. "I found our shelter."

He pulled out his flute and played a song of celebration. He put in lots of extra trills and sweeps. This was the perfect place for them to wait for Mister Elliot.

Chapter 12

SPIKE

AFTER WHAT FELT LIKE an hour, maybe two, as we were approaching the island, I heard something above the hum of the boat motor. A sound drifting out from the rocky cliffs. I listened hard. It was faint music, high-pitched. Pipe music, maybe? Violin? A strange tune.

"What's that music?" I asked the old man. "Where's it coming from?"

Seamus looked back at me blankly. Could be that Seamus was a bit deaf and his old ears couldn't hear the music. Maybe my aunt was playing a CD. But it must be really loud for the sound to carry this far out over the water.

The island looked like the most desolate place you could imagine. Nothing but grey stone cliffs, piles of soggy moss-covered boulders and jagged reefs rising up in the surf along the shore. Where were the trees? The sandy beaches?

The rain had soaked into my coat. I pulled my hood down lower over my forehead.

When we'd almost reached the island, the old man turned the boat to starboard and we travelled with the steep cliffs on our left. The rain was lighter now. More a heavy mist than rain.

"Looks like there isn't a single beach on this whole island," I called out.

"A few hidden ones." He glanced back at me again. "Special places."

"Did my mother ever come to this island?"

"Lela? Yes, she did. She did, indeed. Many years ago she lived here with her family."

"Really? My mother actually lived here? On this island?"

The man nodded. "The Isle of Last Chance is the Beginning Place." He stared into the distance. "When the world was new, all whirling and spinning and the light came shining through the darkness . . ."

I rolled my eyes. "Crazy old dude. Crazy."

As the boat motored around the island, I stared out at its tall cliffs and rain-lashed scrubby bushes. Not exactly your tropical paradise. We must be getting closer to Maureen Calhoun's place. She sure didn't sound enthusiastic over the phone about my coming to her island. She'd probably hate me.

Not that I really cared, I reminded myself, since I wasn't planning on staying long anyway.

We went around a bank of rocks sticking out into the surf and entered a protected bay where the sea suddenly went quiet. It was as if an invisible calming blanket had been spread out over the water. I turned to look back. I couldn't see the mainland at all so now we must be on the opposite side of the island.

A lighthouse came into view. It had been built high on a cliff jutting out into the crashing waves.

Seamus cut the motor and the boat drifted toward a dock until it bounced against the boards of a narrow mooring float. The wooden float was attached to the dock by a sloping ramp. Another boat was moored against the float. A small motorboat with *Sea Quest* painted in fancy black letters on its side.

A hearty-looking woman hurried down the ramp, a welcoming smile creasing her pink cheeks. She had wild grey-streaked hair that looked like it hadn't seen the inside of a hair salon for years. She pulled it away from her face and worked an elastic band onto to it to hold it back.

"Welcome to Last Chance Island. Welcome, Lily. I'm so glad to meet Lela's daughter at last. And just look at you! You're the spit of your dear mother, so you are. Tall, slender. Same dark eyes, elegant eyebrows. I'd know you anywhere." She opened her arms for a hug.

But I brushed her off, ducking away to grab my suitcase.

"Your mother and I grew up together and were great friends," the woman babbled on, still smiling. "But I'm sure your father's told you all about that. Oh, such adventures we had when we were young! Some people said she was a wild one, your mother was, Lily. Always up for an adventure. And she could be a handful for her parents."

"Spike," I grunted, dragging my suitcase over the side of the boat. "The name's Spike."

"Spike? Oh, you want me to call you Spike?"

I nodded.

"All right. Spike, it is." Maureen nodded back. "Well, I must say, you certainly look like a modern city girl with all those rings and the purple hair. A right modern city girl."

I ran my fingers through my damp bangs to lift them away from my forehead, but they flopped back. I felt like setting the woman straight right from the beginning by telling her that Feefee was crazy to send me here to this desolate place, and Maureen was even crazier to agree to take me. And they'd both regret it.

But I didn't bother. What was the point since I wasn't staying here for more than a couple of days anyway? First chance I got, I'd be taking off, back to the mainland, and back to Dublin, meeting up with gorgeous Kieran O'Grady and the other travellers.

"Now, do let me help you with your suitcase." The woman reached out. "Looks heavy, so it does."

"It's OK." I pulled it away. "I've got it. I don't need help."

The woman shook her head and laughed quietly. "It must be hungry and so exhausted you are, after that long journey, all the way from Canada. I have an early tea waiting for you in the kitchen." She turned to the old dude. "Thanks for bringing her, Seamus. We'll be talking to you soon."

"You need anything, you give me a call." He waved to her, untied the boat and put it into reverse to leave the dock. "You too, Lela's girl. You call me when you need to."

I nodded goodbye, glad he wasn't a pirate after all.

Dragging my suitcase through the wind-driven rain, I followed the woman along the dock and up another wooden ramp to a path. The suitcase's wheels dug into the loose sand and made two crooked lines as I tugged it along between the rows of smooth boulders. The path led to a small house, also freshly painted. It squatted beside the tall lighthouse like a pet dog beside his owner.

With the rain-sleeked paint, the whole scene looked like a postcard of a lighthouse and its caretaker's miniature house. Could be any lighthouse anywhere.

So this was Last Chance Island. Wonder why they called it that?

"Come in, Spike. Come in." Maureen led the way into the house. "I'll show you your room."

Pulling my suitcase, I followed her up the steps and inside. We went through a living room, lined with bookshelves, with big old chairs and a sofa, and then into a warm kitchen or family-type room. A hefty wooden table was crowded with magazines, a laptop computer and other tools, so it looked as if it doubled as a workbench and desk. My nose wrinkled at the smell of something with cheese and fish drifting from the oven. Yuck.

Maureen opened a door off a short hallway at the back of the house. "This was our box room but I cleared it out for you and put in a bed. I thought it would be better than sleeping on the sofa in the sitting room. Sorry it's so small though."

The room sure was small, all right, I thought, as I dragged my suitcase past her. It was tiny. Just a closet, really. Barely enough space for the bed, a small lamp table and chair. There wasn't even a mirror where I could check my hair. The rain and waves had washed out the gel so it was hanging down over my eyes and limp as an old dishrag.

"When you're settled, come to the kitchen for a bite of tea," Maureen said.

I nodded through my floppy hair and lifted my suitcase onto the bed. I unzipped it and searched through the clothes, poking with my fingers for my gel. The more I searched, the more peeved I got. Must be in here somewhere.

Then it really hit me. This whole thing was a bloody nightmare. Here I was, miles from anywhere I could buy anything. Not even a stupid tube of gel. I couldn't talk to my friends. Or really do anything. I was literally marooned on this island. Alone.

Not only alone on an island, but alone in my life. Now that my father was gone, I had no family. No one. I was now a family of one.

My heart hammered.

My fingers touched something familiar in my suitcase. My leather pouch. I shook out the silver pocket watch and held its smooth coolness against my cheek. It wasn't ticking. Must have forgotten to wind it last night, so I wound it now, working the tiny knob on its side back and forth until I could hear the whispered tick, tick, tick.

I shut my eyes and listened, breathing deeply until my heart stopped pounding so hard and settled into regular beating.

From the bed I could see through the window to the sea and the waves smashing up against the rocks below the lighthouse. I stared out through the mist, trying to make out the mainland but all I could see was the horizon where the grey sea met the grey sky. So to get back to the mainland, I'll have to go back around the whole island to the other side and head for land that way.

"Come and have something to eat, Spike," Maureen called from the kitchen. "You must be starving, so you must."

"OK," I sighed. I slipped the watch back into the pouch and pulled it around my neck, tucking it inside my shirt. It felt good to keep it close.

I poked deeper into my suitcase and found the gel. Rubbing a dab into my hair, I tried to spike it up with my fingers but it still felt limp. Since I didn't have a mirror to check it out, it'd have to do for now.

I meandered into the kitchen and sat at the scrubbed wooden table, cleared now of computer and books and set with two linen place mats.

"My, that's a different sort of hairdo." Maureen's eyes were wide.

I shrugged. This woman was as back-woodsy as they come.

"Hope you like tuna." She placed a plate with a mound of food in front of me. "Tuna casserole's my regular old stand-by."

I stared down at the food and wrinkled my nose. Tuna casserole had to be my all time least favourite meal. Smelled like a vulture's crotch, but I just said, "Sorry. It's not my fave." And tried not to curl my lip.

Maureen raised her eyebrows. "Too bad, my dear. That's what's for tea today." Her voice sounded dry. Not the least sympathetic. Well, what else had I expected?

"Not really all that hungry." I nibbled a carrot stick.

Maureen sat opposite me at the table. "If that's all you eat, no wonder you're so slim. But your mother was slim too. Maybe that's where you get it. That was a terrible long journey, all the way from Canada. Did they at least feed you on the plane?"

"Not really." I played with the food, pushing the coagulated noodles around the plate. I wanted to ask the woman more about my mother. What kind of girl was she? What did she really look like? Did she live in this very house? What sorts of adventures did they have growing up? But I didn't.

Instead I muttered, "So what's there to do for excitement around here?"

"Not a lot for a young person, I'm afraid. I'm not sure this is going to work out, having you here." Maureen shook her head. "You'll find it so different from living in a city. I don't know what you'll be doing all day. Do you like reading?"

"Not so much."

"Well, if you did, we have a pretty good selection of books here. During the day, I'm busy with the lighthouse. It takes a lot of work to keep it functioning, oiling all the machinery, checking the settings, monitoring incoming boats on the radio. Even at night sometimes, when those north winds come up, or the fog's so thick it's like your head's in a paper bag, and I've got to activate the fog horn and keep watch for any boats capsizing. Maintaining this lighthouse is a full-time job. Especially now Gerry's gone and I have to do it all myself."

"Gerry?"

"My husband. Didn't your father tell you that he died last Christmas?"

I shook my head.

"Heart attack. Same as your father. I was sorry to hear about that, love. It's hard to lose a parent when you're young."

"Yeah." I nodded. "Um, thanks."

She smiled and patted my arm.

I reached for another carrot stick and we ate in silence for a while. Then she said, "For evening's entertainment here, there's the television but we get only two channels and sometimes the reception isn't so great."

"I've got my tablet so I can do stuff on that. What's your access code?"

"Tablet? Access code?"

"Yeah, your access code so I can hook up to your Internet."

"Oh, that's what you're talking about. Sorry, but I have just a phone hook-up."

"For your laptop?"

"Right. It has to be connected to the phone to get access to the Internet. But I do that just for emergencies because it's a long distance call. Anyway, when I go to into town I can take my laptop and check my emails at the public library."

"What? No Internet here? How can you live without the net?"

"I do a lot of reading."

"You said no one else is living here on the whole island?"

"Only me now," Maureen said. "Looking after the lighthouse has been in the family for generations, but everyone else is gone. All we have for company are the seals that come up onto the rocks to sun themselves, and of course, gulls and cormorants. And sometimes, the odd eagle."

"Seals, gulls, cormorants and odd eagles." I nodded, running my fingers through my hair again, lifting it away from my eyes. How fantastically exciting can you get.

Oh well, I wasn't sticking around long anyway, I reminded myself again.

Chapter 13

KALU

KALU AND AISHA SPENT most of the day in the cave, high up on the cliff, out of the rain and wind, and away from the pounding surf. The cave was cozy but far from warm. By late afternoon, although it was still misty, it had stopped raining so they slid back down the mossy cliff to the beach.

Aisha's nose was running. She sniffed and wiped it on her tattered shawl.

Kalu's stomach rumbled with hunger, and he was chilly.

"How about a fire?" he asked his cousin.

"Yes. Let's make one."

She helped him build a sort of shelter from the wind out of rocks. Kalu tried to start the fire. He thought it would be easy with the matches in his bag. He wouldn't have to twirl a stick onto another piece of wood the way his uncles usually started a fire. But he was wrong. The wind blew out one match after another before it could ignite the mound of grass and twigs he'd piled in the shelter.

Aisha sat on the rock beside him and watched. Her plastic bag cape crinkled as she stretched out her legs. "How about using the plastic bag to shield your fire from the wind?" She pulled off her cape and arranged it around the rocks.

"OK, and I'll see if I can find something dryer than this grass." Kalu searched the crevices in the cliff and came up with a handful of dried moss and leaves. He also found a few more twigs that snapped when he bent them. A good sign they were dry.

He tried again, striking a match and coaxing the small flame with the moss. Then he fed the flame with the dry twigs and some thin branches. He blew gently to encourage the flames, and this time they were lucky. Soon a small fire was crackling between the rocks. He grinned at Aisha and she smiled her gap-toothed smile back at him. It felt great warming their hands and toes. They toasted the end of the loaf of bread on a stick.

Aisha showed Kalu how to open the tin of sardines with the special key stuck to its bottom.

"I didn't know you could do that," he marvelled.

"Mister Elliot showed me. Do you think he'll be back this afternoon to pick us up?"

"He might be. Or tomorrow, for sure, I bet."

They took turns dipping the crusty bits of bread into the sardine tin, mopping up every last drop of fish and oil with their fingers.

"Mmm. Good supper." Kalu smacked his lips.

Aisha's nose was dripping even more now, and she coughed and coughed. Without her plastic cape to cut the wind, she was shivering again.

"Maybe you should go back up to the cave out of the wind where it's warmer," Kalu suggested. "And take the plastic."

"What about the fire?" Aisha yawned then coughed some more.

"We've had supper. We don't need it anymore. And maybe sleep is the best thing for you to get better."

While Aisha curled up and slept in the cave under the plastic bag, Kalu pulled out his wooden flute. He leaned against the cliff and blew into it. He played all the tunes he could think of, remembering the evenings around the fire in his village. He played sad tunes, thinking about his family, his uncles, his brother, and his mother. About all the people in his village that were lost. That he'd never see again.

When he ran out of tunes, he made some up, experimenting with trills and booms. He played his flute the rest of the evening to the wind and the water, the moss and the bushes. He played until his heart was full.

Before dusk came he realized that he wouldn't be able to see the sun setting and play the good night song to it on his flute. The sun was moving across the sky to the other side of the island. It would be setting on the other side of the tall cliffs.

He climbed up to the cave to check on Aisha. She was in a deep sleep curled up under the plastic bag. He stared out to sea. There was no sign of Mister Elliot's boat so maybe it would be safe to leave for a while. He wondered if there was a trail that would take him to the other side of the island.

"Aisha," he whispered. "I'm just going to see the sunset. You'll be OK?"

Her eyes fluttered open and she nodded. Then she closed them, and with a deep sigh she fell back asleep.

In the long shadows, Kalu saw the faint trail travelling from their cave, up and over the steep cliff and through some short purple bushes. It was hard going but it took him higher on the island until he'd climbed to the top and he could see the ocean on the other side. The sun was low in the sky now. He would have to hurry to reach the other side of the island before it set. The trail levelled out and meandered through thin bushes and stunted trees back and forth until it started to descend, switchbacking down a steep cliff.

About halfway down the cliff, he stopped. Perched on a rocky cliff down by the beach was the oddest building he'd ever seen. It was enormously tall, but so narrow, it was no wider than the huts in his village. The top was made of windows, and every now and then, there was a flash of bright light. So very strange.

But he had to hurry. The sun was dropping lower and

lower on the horizon. He crept toward the tall building. It seemed deserted. No one was around.

The outer rim of the sun was just reaching the edge of the sea, spraying out a golden path on the water. He climbed over the rocks to the water's edge, lifted his bamboo flute to his lips and blew the good night tune.

He played and played, wishing the sun a safe journey through the night until tomorrow.

Chapter 14

SPIKE

AFTER SUPPER WHILE MAUREEN went to check shortwave radio messages in the lighthouse, I pushed open the small bedroom window at the back of the house and leaned out. I pulled in a deep breath of cold salty air and stared at the orange sun sinking toward the horizon, dragging a long orange path on the sea. The water was calm now, hardly a ripple, and wind had blown away the mist. The evening breeze ruffled the curtains, blowing in sounds of water lapping and gulls screeching overhead.

It was faint at first, but now I was sure I heard something else. That weird music. Same music I'd heard on Seamus's boat. High-pitched notes. Violin, maybe? Or flute? I couldn't tell. Where was it coming from? The lighthouse? The woman must be playing a CD of new-age melodies out there.

I shivered and started to close the window. But I noticed movement in the bushes near the water's edge on the other side of the lighthouse. I stared.

Was that a person? Yes! Not Maureen for sure. A boy, maybe? Tall, thin, wearing ragged cut-offs and a t-shirt. He was a silhouette against the sky lit by the last rays of the setting sun.

But Maureen had just said no one else lived on the island. Just her. So who could that be? Weird!

The figure crept over the rocks as if he were trying to hide. Then he stood up behind a big boulder where I could still see him, shading his eyes and watching the sun sink down into the water in a blaze of purple and gold and orange.

He lifted something to his mouth. Something long and thin. A whistle or a flute, maybe? So that's where the music must have been coming from.

I ran through the house and out the front door, slamming it behind me. I dashed around the house to the back. But now I couldn't see him. I searched the rocks down beside the waves, but there was no sign of him. He'd disappeared.

Where had he gone? Who was that boy? Where'd he come from? What was he doing here? And hadn't Maureen heard his music?

Later, when Maureen returned from the lighthouse, I was going to ask her about him. But by then I was so sleepy it was just too much effort.

For an instant when I woke up the next morning, I was surprised to find I was lying in a tangle of sheets beneath the duvet on a narrow bed in a tiny room. Right. Last Chance. I rubbed my eyes and crawled out, pulling on jeans and a t-shirt from my suitcase on the floor.

In the bathroom across the hall I splashed water on my face and stared at my hair in the mirror above the sink. At least the purple dye was lasting, I thought, as I ran my fingers through the wiry bangs. The bangs flopped forward over my eyes. The gel was crap. I should have brought along some stronger stuff.

I wandered into the kitchen thinking about the boy I'd seen on the rocks last night. I opened my mouth to ask Maureen about him. But for some reason I changed my mind.

Maureen was sitting at the table, thumbing through a magazine and listening to an iPod with earphones. She was eating a bowl of porridge and sliced apples.

"Oh!" She pulled off the earphones. "You startled me, Lily. I hope you slept all right. Were you warm enough? That was some wind. Hope it didn't keep you awake. Help yourself to a cup of tea if you like."

I poured myself some tea from the pot on the counter and sighed. "The name's Spike." How many times would I have to remind her?

"Sorry, Spike." Maureen bit her lip. "I'll try to remember. How can you see with your hair down over your eyes like that? Want me to trim it a wee bit for you?"

"No thanks." I flipped it back. "I like it this way."

Maureen shook her head. "What about breakfast? Porridge? Toast and marmalade?"

"Not really that hungry." I took a banana from the fruit bowl. Bruised on the bottom so I dropped it back, glancing at Maureen who was writing on a pad of paper beside her bowl now. "Shopping list?" I asked.

"No. A list of reasons why my job here is essential on the island."

"Why do you need that?"

"The Commissioners of Irish Lights is sending over some people to look at our whole operation. They're talking about shutting me down and automating our lighthouse, especially now that Gerry's gone . . ." Her voice wobbled and she blew her nose.

"Commissioners of Irish Lights?"

She cleared her throat. "They're sort of government people who hired Gerry and me years ago to look after the light."

"Wouldn't it be better for everyone if the whole thing were automated?"

"Certainly not. If we weren't here, many boats would come to grief. Not only do we keep the light in the lighthouse operating twenty-four hours a day, but we also broadcast changes in the weather, the winds and waves out to the mariners. And we activate the foghorn when it's foggy. Sometimes storms come in from the west with no warning. If we weren't here to tell boaters about them, there'd be many more shipwrecks on those reefs."

I stifled a yawn as the woman rattled on. "I promised Gerry I'd stay on here as long as I could. It was his dying wish. You see, if a boat ever capsizes or crashes out on the reefs, I can call straight away to the coast guard for a search and rescue. Or maybe even go out in my boat to rescue them if they're not too far out. Now that's something an automated light-house could never do."

"So when are the Commissioner guys coming?"

"They called last night that they'd be here this morning. In fact, they'll probably be here soon. They like to start work at dawn's crack."

Dawn's crack? I laughed inside. She must mean the crack of dawn. I put my tea on the table and sat opposite her. "But how can you stand living way out here on the island by your-self, day after day? There's nothing to do. No one to talk to."

"Ah, girl. Livin' on an island's the best sort of life you can have. For me anyway. I love it, the freedom of it all. Especially here on Last Chance. Also just knowing how grateful the boaters are gives me lots of job satisfaction. Beats working in a stuffy old supermarket any day."

"Doesn't look like much fun to me."

"Exactly what I told your father's, um, friend, Miss McPhee, so I did." She shook her head. "Island life's not much of a life for a young person. I hope you'll find enough to do to occupy yourself here. Now are you sure you don't want any porridge?"

I screwed up my nose.

"Well, that's breakfast this morning."

"OK, I guess," I sighed. I didn't want to admit my stomach had been growling since I woke up, especially since I hadn't eaten much last night.

"It's on the stove. Help yourself."

I took a bowl to the stove and plopped some porridge into it from the pot. "Hope you've got brown sugar?"

"Brown sugar, and cream too, if you like. After breakfast I could give you a tour of the lighthouse before the government men arrive."

"Sure," I sighed, slurping a spoonful of the gluey cereal. "I guess."

I thought the lighthouse tour was going to be the most boring ever, but it turned out to be actually really interesting.

After climbing the steep inside spiral staircase to the top of the narrow building, Maureen showed me how the brightness of the lamp was magnified by these really cool prisms built into big windows around the top of the lighthouse. The prisms made the lamp so bright and powerful, its light shot through the morning mist into the sea like a shotgun bullet.

Squeaky and humming machinery — all levers and pulleys — pivoted the lamp so the beam could sweep around the top of the tall building. Sort of like the insides of a clock, but magnified hundreds of times. Noisy but way cool.

"Would you mind polishing the windows for me?" Maureen handed me a squirt bottle and leather chamois. She had to raise her voice over the machinery's thumping and squeaking. "I want everything perfect when the inspectors arrive."

"Sure. What's in the bottle?" Smelled familiar.

"Just a drop of vinegar and water. Works great if you use enough elbow grease." Maureen dabbed some oil into the moving parts around the big lamp and tightened some screws. "The window prisms work best when they're kept sparkling clean. I'll have to climb up the ladders to clean the outsides. Those pesky gulls like to use the lighthouse for target practice."

After she'd tinkered with the lighthouse mechanism, and I'd finished giving all the inside of the windows a quick polish, Maureen looked around the room. "That will have to do for now." She put her tools away into a narrow closet at the top of the stairs. "Bring the chamois and squirt bottle down and I'll attack those outside windows."

Power for the lighthouse lamp and its moving parts came from a generator housed near the door in an enclosure at the bottom of the winding stairs that she pointed out to me on our way down. "But I don't know how long this old generator's going to last. It's on its last legs and, if it goes, there'll be no power for our lights in the house. But even more important, no power for the lighthouse lamp. And in the middle of a stormy night, that could be fatal for any boaters out there." She stopped to adjust a loose connection on the rusty old machine.

"That generator's so old and rusty it's amazing it still works," I said.

"You're so right. The sooner we get a new one, the better."

The generator wasn't only rusty but the dials and handles, as well as the hoses, were taped up with so much duct tape, it looked more duct tape than generator.

"The main thing is not to run out of fuel," she said. "If that ever happens, it's a dickens to restart the motor."

"How do you do that?"

"First thing, you get the fuel going in again. That's through this hose. Then, see this tap right here?" She pointed to a tap painted red near the top. "It's a purge valve. You have to turn it like this, then press the starter button here." The starter button was also red and had "start" painted above it. "Anyway, if you forget, there are instructions on this decal."

I followed Maureen outside through a wide doorway.

She turned back. "One thing we must always remember is to shut this door firmly and put the door latch on."

I tried not to roll my eyes, but by now I sure was getting tired of her lectures.

"If we don't latch it properly," she went on, "the wind could blow the door open and rain would drench everything in sight including this handy device right here." She pointed to a black plastic box about the size of a lunch box just inside the door, with heavy wires snaking out of it and into the ceiling.

"What's that?"

"Our emergency power. It has extra batteries in there. If the generator fails, and it never has yet on my watch, the batteries will kick in and power the lamp for a few hours. At least until we get the generator mended." After latching the door securely, she hitched the spray bottle into her belt and threw the chamois over her shoulder. She smiled at me as she put her hand on the ladder attached to the outside of the lighthouse.

"I could do that," I offered. "Clean the windows up there." It'd give me something to do. Maybe I'd be high enough to see across the island and get a glimpse of how far the mainland was from here.

But Maureen shook her head. "Thanks, love, but it's too high and dangerous, climbing with your hands full. Your dear father, may he rest in peace, wouldn't be very happy if you fell and broke your neck on your first day here, now would he."

"Humph," I grunted. The thought of my father looking down from somewhere up in those clouds caused a sinking feeling in my stomach. Like my insides were filled with rocks and weighing me down. I'd never, ever see him again.

To stop myself from blubbering like a baby, I picked up some pebbles by the door and tossed them hard, one by one, into the waves splashing around the edge of the big rocks at the base of the lighthouse. After a while my arm got tired.

Maybe I could explore around the place. As I climbed down toward the water, the small motorboat I'd noticed yesterday, came into view. It was still tied to the mooring float, bouncing lightly against the boards.

"What about the motorboat?" I called back over the wind to Maureen when she came down the ladder. "Can I take it out for a spin? I've driven my father's boat around Lake Ontario tons of times and it's a really big one, a 40-foot catamaran, so I wouldn't have any trouble with that outboard. I'll even keep a PFD on the whole entire time."

But Maureen shook her head, as she shouted back. "I'd really rather you waited until later, after the inspectors have come and gone. Then I'll be happy to take you exploring. I could show you some pretty little bays and inlets around the island. How about this evening? Maybe we could even take a picnic for our tea. By then the winds will probably have died down so it won't be such a bumpy boat ride."

I frowned and kicked at a rock. Bummer.

"There's a trail on the other side of the lighthouse that goes around the cliff and leads up to a great lookout," Maureen continued. "Highest point of the island, so on a clear day you have a 360-degree view of not only the sea out here, but back to the mainland as well. You could explore that if you fancy a bit of exercise."

Hiking up a stupid hill. Not exactly a bowlful of fun. I kept frowning.

"Maybe you could find a book to read inside then. You're welcome to whatever you fancy. Also help yourself to some fruit if you get peckish."

I turned away and wandered along the trail to the house with my hands deep in my jeans pockets. God! Absolutely nothing to do here. Friggin' desolate lump of rock was right.

Maureen wouldn't let me take out the motorboat alone today. Or probably ever.

Then a thought hit me that started my heart racing. If I was going to escape from this dismal place, I'd have to just take the boat without her permission.

Sooner, the better. Yes!

First chance I get, I'll grab it . . .

Chapter 15

KALU

THE MORNING SUN'S RAYS broke through the bush in front of the shallow cave where Kalu and his small cousin were sleeping. He stretched out his legs and moved the branches aside to stare out at the water. No boats out there as far as he could see. Not a single one. Mister Elliot still hadn't arrived to pick them up.

Maybe he wouldn't ever come back. But Kalu pushed that thought right out of his head.

Aisha woke up coughing, a deep hacking cough. He gave her the water bottle. There was just a bit of water left at the bottom. He should have tried to collect some last night when it was raining.

She sipped the water and stopped coughing. "Mister Elliot?" she asked. Her voice was husky.

"Not yet," he said. "Are you hungry? There are a few crackers left in the box."

After they'd nibbled the crackers and licked up all the crumbs from the package, Kalu was still hungry.

"Maybe I could catch a fish," he said. "Then we could cook it on the fire. That would be delicious, right?"

"Right." Aisha yawned and her eyelids looked heavy.

"You stay here. I'll go catch us some lunch."

Kalu didn't have a fishing line or even a hook, but maybe, if he was very fast, he could catch a fish with his bare hands. Shouldn't be that hard.

He squatted at the edge of the clear water and waited, staring down into it. After a while, a school of tiny fish flitted by in the shallow water. Quick as a blink, he tried to scoop up some in his hands, but they skittered away like silver lightning.

Was there anything he could use to catch them? A net? He looked around the beach. Right. The sardine tin from their meal yesterday was beside their fire pit. He got it and stood in deeper water now, halfway up to his knees, holding the tin ready. The water was so cold his feet throbbed, but he stood as still as a rock, waiting.

Soon a small crab arrived waving its long legs and nibbled at his toes with its claw, tickling him. He felt like shaking it off, but he didn't move. Then another crab crawled by and chased away the first. But still no fish came.

There were some shells attached to the rocks at the water's edge. Kalu pulled one off. It was dark blue and there was probably something to eat inside. He tried pulling the shell apart but it was locked shut. If only he had a knife, maybe he'd be able to pry it open.

As he collected a bunch of the shellfish in the sardine tin, a round shape popped up in the water close to shore. It was a sea creature they had seen earlier from Mister Elliot's boat.

"Seals," he'd told them. "Nothing but pests. They like to come and nibble at my catch in the net."

Another seal popped up. And another. The seals stared at Kalu with curious brown eyes.

"Hello, seals," he called, staring back at them.

They twitched their whiskers and dived back into the water. Kalu carried the sardine tin of shellfish to the fire pit. While he was gathering some dried moss and sticks to build a fire, Aisha called him from the cave. "Is lunch ready now?"

"Soon. I'm just making a fire."

She slithered down the cliff and watched while he made the fire. This time he got it going quite quickly using only two matches from his denim bag. He stored the bag under a rock so it wouldn't blow away.

"Did you catch a fish?" she asked him.

"No fish, but I found some shells that must have something tasty inside."

She took one from the tin and tried to pry the shells apart. "How do you open them?"

"I don't know, but maybe if we put them on the fire?"

Once the fire was going well, he laid a few of the purple shells on top.

"Look," Aisha said. "You're right. That one's popped open."

Kalu poked the opened shell out of the fire with a stick. "You want to try it first?" he asked, carefully pulling the hot shell apart, revealing a small grey lump about the size of his thumb.

Aisha shook her head and sniffed, wiping her nose on her ragged shawl. "No, you."

"OK, here goes." He popped the morsel into his mouth. It tasted like a warm bit of salty fish. "Mmm. Delicious," he said, reaching for another that had popped open as well. "You have to try one."

Aisha agreed that the little shellfish were delicious and she ate a couple more before starting to cough. Her nose was really running and her eyes looked heavy. The wind had come up and she shivered.

"Maybe you should go back up to the cave out of the wind," he told her.

She nodded and slowly climbed back up the cliff.

By the time Kalu finished eating some more of the shell-fish, the fire had died down. The wind was blowing right onto the beach now, and the water had come in quite far so sometimes the wind blew the waves right up beside their fire pit. He shivered and decided to climb up to the cave with the remaining shellfish for Aisha. They had a good view of the sea from there to watch for Mister Elliot.

He should be here soon.

Chapter 16

SPIKE

I WANDERED DOWN TO the rocks near the water. A couple of dark heads bounced in the waves near the shore. They turned whiskered faces to stare at me with these huge brown eyes. Must be the seals Maureen had mentioned. Their faces, with their staring eyes, were so human-like, they looked as if they could almost speak.

"Hallo!" I called out to them. They kept on staring. I wondered what they were thinking about. I stared back, playing the game of who'd blink first.

But I soon got chilled by the wind so I turned away and wandered up to the house to check Maureen's books. Mostly old classics like *David Copperfield* and Jane Austen with a sprinkling of detective novels and travel books.

One book looked sort of interesting. *The Secret of Roan Inish*. I flipped through it and found it was about Selkies. Kind of disguised seals that lived on remote islands around Scotland and Ireland. Islands like Last Chance, I thought.

If the time was right, they could climb out of the water, shed their furry coats and assume human forms. Sometimes they even married islanders and had children and lived with them for years before returning to their watery homes. How bizarre was that!

I turned the pages and read about one beautiful Selkie who'd done just that.

The seals were always watching her from the sea while sea birds wheeled above her, calling to her in a language she seemed to understand, for often she'd call out a reply that would set them laughing the way gulls do . . .

I remembered the boy I'd seen last night creeping around the rocks below the lighthouse and shivers flicked up my back. Maybe he was a Selkie! Maybe those seals I'd just seen were searching for him to try to lure him back into the water. Or maybe they were trying to hypnotize me and lure *me* into the sea.

Yeah, right. Get real, I told myself.

The sound of a boat's motor interrupted my thoughts. I dropped the book on the coffee table and went outside along the path to see who it was. Away in the distance a powerful-looking boat was spraying out a high plume of water as it made a beeline for Maureen's dock.

She hurried along the path past the house. "Mary, Mother of God and all the saints in heaven! Here they are already. The inspectors." She anxiously pulled her hair back into her elastic band. "Come to decide if Last Chance Light will be run by Maureen Calhoun or by a computer."

A nervous smile plastered on her face, she rushed down to the dock to greet the inspectors while I wandered back into the house and into the closet I'd been given as a bedroom. I flung myself onto the bed and stared up at the ceiling. A crack ran crookedly across it from one corner to the other where a spider's web trembled in a draft. Man, was this place ever bo-ring!

Wait! Just a minute! I sat up so fast I knocked over the lamp.

This was my chance! While Maureen was busy with the government guys in the lighthouse, here was my chance to get away. To escape from this mega-boring place.

I'd need a few things. Important things like money. I could stuff everything into my backpack. Euros I got at the airport. My mother's watch, for sure. Change of clothes. And of course, the Visa card my father had given me last Christmas. "Just for emergencies," he'd said.

I'll take Maureen's little motorboat across the water over to Skibb-whatever. Then hop a cab to the train station where I'll catch the train to Dublin. Good thing I knew the route.

Once I got to Dublin, I'll meet up with gorgeous Kieran and his friends again. If they were still away I'd just wait for them at the squat down by the canal. They were all so friendly. Like I was already part of their gang. I remembered that warm glow of belonging.

Yay, yay, I grinned to myself, dancing around the room. Could hardly wait.

I heard Maureen talking to the inspector guys as they wandered up to the house. I glanced out the window to see two of them, both dressed in identical navy uniforms. The older man with grey hair and a jaunty walk talked in a loud, commanding voice to Maureen as she led them past the house to the lighthouse. Another dude, younger, plumper, scooted along behind, loaded down with briefcases and boxes.

Tweedle Dee and Tweedle Dumb.

Maureen would be busy for a while now, showing the inspector dudes around the lighthouse and all her records and stuff.

After packing my backpack with essentials, I pulled it over my shoulder and slipped out of the bedroom. Maybe I should grab some food to last me until I could buy some on the mainland. Piece of cheese from the fridge. Half a loaf of bread from the cupboard. Couple of oranges from the fruit bowl. I loaded up a plastic grocery bag and forced the bag into my pack on top of the clothes.

I glanced out the kitchen window. No sign of Maureen or the inspector dudes now. Must be inside the lighthouse, checking it out. I had to get away before they finished. I could probably start the boat by hot-wiring the motor, but it'd be faster if I had the key. Where would Maureen keep it?

Hooks beside the door held bunches of keys. Car key, house keys. One with a coiled red wire attached. Looked like what my father used for his boat. Key to Maureen's boat, maybe? What the heck. I grabbed a handful. Boat key's got to be one of them. I shoved them all into my jacket pocket.

I crept down the outside steps and along the path that led to the ramp, half expecting Maureen to call out, asking where I was heading. But so far, so good.

When I reached the dock, I glanced back at the lighthouse. Unless Maureen and the men were staring out the windows in this direction, they wouldn't see me. I fumbled as I worked to untie the knot in the boat's painter. There. Finally got it undone.

I tossed in my pack and scrambled to the stern where I stuck the key with the red coil into the motor and pressed the starter button. The motor coughed into life. Yay! 35-horsepower Yamaha four-stroke. Could use oil and maybe a spark-plug cleaning, but no time for that. Had to get away. Now.

I shoved it into gear and the boat pulled away from the dock.

The motor wasn't fast enough to pull a water-skier, but plenty powerful enough for this small boat with only me in it. Teeth chattering with excitement, I checked what was in the boat. Bits of rope and a plastic pail for a bailer were shoved under the bow. Good. PFD under the rear seat. I dug it out and pulled it on, cinching it tightly around my middle.

I'd need it if the boat capsized or got swamped. Swimming wasn't exactly my strong suit. Besides, it'd cut the wind so it wouldn't blow through to my bones.

I steered the runabout out of the protected bay and turned to starboard. At first, in the lea of the island, the water was calm and the boat's bow sliced through rippling waves. But as the wind picked up, the waves grew bigger and rougher. Soon whitecaps were hitting the boat's hull, splashing over the gunnels.

The further I ventured away from the island, the rougher the waves became, splashing in even more water. One huge wave bashed against the boat's hull. The boat tipped sideways and gulped up seawater. My insides lurched with fear.

Maybe heading straight across the bay to the mainland when the water was so rough wasn't such a good plan. Pulling on the tiller I turned the boat to hug the edge of the island. Should be quieter in the lee.

But it wasn't. In fact, in just a few minutes, the wind had really picked up. It blew froth from the tips of whitecaps onto my cheeks. Tasted salty on my lips.

But no way was I turning back to the lighthouse now. This might be my one and only chance to escape from that island prison.

As waves bashed against the boat, I kept it hugging the shore. I realized that I needed a breather until the wind and waves calmed down. Where could I land? So far, only steep cliffs and huge rocks with this crazy frothy surf crashing all over the place. No way could I land here. I squeezed the tiller, kept the boat moving forward, slowly now. Slowly. Tried to climb up the front of the waves and slide down into the troughs.

And concentrated on not panicking.

"Stay calm. Stay calm. Stay friggin' calm," I muttered as the boat lurched sideways. My heart was pounding practically out of my chest. I could hardly breathe.

A beach had to be around here somewhere.

Yes! A break in the cliff face. Narrow inlet just ahead. I jerked the motor speed down to a crawl. Steered the boat behind a jagged reef. A tiny beach.

Wind and waves suddenly dropped. I gulped in relief.

I switched off the motor and tilted it out of the water so the prop wouldn't scrape the bottom. The boat drifted to shore until its aluminum hull crunched on the gravelly beach.

Out of the direct wind and waves it was so much calmer. I pulled off the PFD. Whew! Those waves were monstrous! My heart still pounded like mad. I pulled in a deep breath and kicked off my shoes and tied them around my neck. After rolling up my jeans, I grabbed my backpack, climbed over the gunnels and landed knee-deep in clear water. My feet stung with cold as I splashed to the beach and took another deep breath. Man, did it feel good to be on solid land again.

I sat on a rock and tied my shoes back on. Then took a look around at the bushes and rocks and cliffs and water.

So, here I was, still on this stupid island. Now what?

Chapter 17

KALU

IN THE CAVE KALU'S doze was interrupted by the sound of a boat motor.

"He's here." He shook Aisha awake. "Mister Elliot's come for us."

Her eyes opened instantly and she squealed with happiness and relief.

But when Kalu parted the bush in front of the cave entrance, he saw it wasn't Mister Elliot after all. It was a small motorboat that had stopped at their beach.

"Shh. Be very quiet," he warned Aisha. "It's not him. It's someone else. Maybe they've come to get us. You know. The coast guard."

Aisha's eyes were huge as she shrank away into the back of the cave.

Kalu watched through the bushes as a girl with long legs climbed out of the boat and waded to shore.

She sat on a rock and put her shoes on, then looked around. She seemed to be searching for something. Maybe for them! But she looked very young to be a coast guard or a police officer. Also she wasn't wearing a uniform. Just jeans and a black jacket.

She stopped at their fire pit and felt the ashes. They'd still be warm so she would know someone had a fire there not so long ago. He should have swept away the evidence of their fire. She poked at their sardine tin with a stick, flipping it over.

Could she really be searching for him and Aisha? Maybe she was just out on a boat ride. But if she found them, she'd report them to the authorities, for sure.

She was tall, maybe even as tall as Kalu was himself, and slender, but not thin. When she pulled off her hat, he saw that her bristly hair was a strange colour. Sort of black with purple all in the front. He'd never seen people with that colour of hair before. And she had a gold ring that went through one of her nostrils. And another through her eyebrow.

She was searching around their fire pit and found his bag with the matches under the rock. Now she was opening it and dumping out his rocks and the matches.

Why had he left it down there? It was a dead giveaway that he and Aisha were hiding close by. He shook his head at his own stupidity.

She called out, as if she were checking if anyone was around.

Of course he didn't answer.

Now she was opening her pack and taking out an orange. As she peeled it and ate it, section by section, his mouth watered and his stomach rumbled with hunger.

What he'd give for just one small taste of that juicy fruit. Aisha was staring hungrily at the orange as well. She sniffed and wiped her runny nose on her shirt. They'd finished eating all the food they'd brought in the plastic bag from Mister Elliot's boat, and so far Kalu's attempts to catch fish had been a dismal failure except for those tiny shellfish. They were even out of fresh water now.

He swallowed. His throat was dry and scratchy.

If Mister Elliot didn't come for them soon with fresh supplies, he didn't know what they would do.

Chapter 18

SPIKE

NO TREES ON THIS part of the island, I noticed, just a few bushes between the rocky cliffs. A faint path led away from the water up to higher ground. I followed it and came across what looked like the remains of a campfire built against a flat rock. Maybe boaters had stopped here for a break and to make lunch? I felt the ashes. Still warm, so the boaters must have been here not long ago. Probably this morning. They'd left a sardine tin behind too. I poked it with a stick.

I noticed a string dangling from under a rock beside the fire pit. I nudged the rock over with my foot and saw the string was attached to a small bag. Strange! Reminded me a bit of my mother's watch pouch. This one was made roughly of a piece of worn denim, drawn together with a bit of grubby string.

I dumped out the contents. Smooth pebbles and a glassy rock that caught the light. Not much of value. I stuck my finger into the bag, searching for anything else. Couple of wooden matches and some dried bits of leaves that stuck in my fingernails. They smelled spicy, like dried basil maybe? I put everything back into the bag and looked around. Whose was it? What should I do with it?

While I was trying to decide, an idea flashed into my head. That figure I'd seen last night on the other side of the lighthouse. That boy. Could there be a connection? As if in answer, I spied a footprint of a bare foot in the sand beside the fire pit.

Not far was another footprint. They both looked fresh.

Someone must be here! Strange! Maureen had said that since her husband had died, she was alone on the island. No one else lived here, she'd said.

Could there be a trail connecting this side of the island to the lighthouse side?

"Hello!" I called out. "Anyone here? Hello?"

No one answered except a bird landing on the high cliff. It squawked back at me then flapped its big wings and flew away. I searched around the cliff base but didn't see anyone or any other evidence. Not a scrap of paper or even other footprints. Also, the faint path stopped at the blank wall of the cliff that rose straight up in front of me. Didn't lead any-where. Certainly not to the other side of the island. Sure was a mystery.

I stuck the denim bag back under the same rock and took another careful look around. Nothing here. Just more stupid rocks and moss and scrubby bush.

I sat on the flat rock. It had been warmed by the sun. As I pulled out an orange from my pack, the pouch with my mother's watch tumbled out. Picking it up, I thought that when she was living on this island years ago, she'd probably explored every inch of it. Maybe she'd even sat right here on this very rock. How cool was that.

Sure wish I'd brought along my tool kit. I hadn't taken the watch apart for a while. I loved doing that. It was like solving a complicated puzzle. Also, whenever I did it, I somehow felt closer to my mother, so on this rock would have been the perfect place to do it.

I shook the watch out of its pouch and held it to my ear, listening hard. Tick, tick, tick. I gazed at its face. The Roman numerals told me it was already past noon. No wonder I was hungry. I pushed the watch back into its pouch and laid it on the rock beside the bag of food while I peeled the orange.

As I was sucking in the tangy juice, my back prickled. I had a strange sensation I was being watched. Was it the Selkies I'd read about? But when I scanned the waves, no round faces of seals were staring at me.

The sun was past high noon and making its way through

billowy clouds toward the western horizon now. I should get going but it looked as if the winds were even stronger now. I could see how they blew up whitecaps on the water. Far in the distance I could make out the dark misty outline of the foothills on the mainland. But there were plenty of danger-ous whitecaps between here and there.

I had to decide real quick. Should I stay here and wait until the winds died down and the sea was calmer, then dash across to the mainland? Or go back to Maureen's place and wait for another day to escape? A day when the winds were calm enough so I'd be able to cross the bay in the small boat safely without it totally capsizing.

Just camping out here by myself at this end of the island and waiting until the sea calmed would be stupid. I didn't have any shelter or even a sleeping bag.

But travelling across the bay to the mainland in this weather would be even stupider. The boat would soon get swamped by the waves and totally sink. I wouldn't last more than some minutes in the freezing water, even wearing the PFD. *Brrr.* Just thinking about it started me shivering.

I glanced up and noticed the boat bouncing around in the waves. It was starting to float away! I snatched up my pack, splashed through thigh-deep water and grabbed the boat before it drifted further out. Tide must be coming in. I clam-bered in over the gunnels. Now my shoes and jeans were soaked. I should have tied up the stupid boat. How irrespon-sible. It could have drifted away. Then what? I'd be stuck here.

Oh well, guess I'll head back to the lighthouse. Bummer.

Maureen will probably blow her top at me for taking her boat after she'd specifically told me not to. But it wouldn't be the first time someone was really mad at me.

What's the worst thing she could do? Never speak to me again and stick me on the next plane back home to Ontario? Well, that'd be just fine with me.

I'd left the lunch bag on the beach but there was no point going back for it. I'd be back at the lighthouse soon enough, and she'd probably have a meal ready.

Besides, I had that prickly feeling at the back of my neck again, of being watched. Creepy. I just wanted to get out of there.

I lowered the motor into the water, pushed in the key and pressed the starter button. The motor came alive with a peppy hum. I pushed it into reverse and backed out of the narrow inlet. The water was even choppier now and the wind whipped my hair around my face. I clenched the tiller and turned the boat, steering it into the frothy waves.

Man, was it rough going. Wall-to-wall whitecaps even close to land now.

If I hugged the edge of the island, in its lee, where the wind wasn't as strong and the waves weren't as high, I should be OK. That's what I told myself, anyway. But as each wave bashed the hull and jolted the boat, my heart lurched.

I glanced at the island on my left now. Rocky cliffs jutted straight down into foamy waves. If the boat sank here, there was absolutely no ledge I could hang onto, to crawl out of the water. Yikes! Just had to make darn sure this boat didn't sink.

A bunch of big whitecaps rolled toward me and battered the hull. I slowed the motor right down until I was creeping past the steep cliffs.

Travelling against the bitter wind and heavy waves, it felt as if the trip back to the lighthouse was ten times longer than coming out. Felt as if the boat was being bashed around, like, forever. Crash, crash. Then I passed another headland and saw the sweeping beam from the lighthouse. Yay! Lighthouse meant safety. Almost there now. Come on, come on.

A gigantic wave bashed against the boat. I gasped as it dumped frigid water over the gunnels, drenching my jeans. Water sloshed around up to my ankles now. The motor coughed and spitted. Now what?

Gas. I was in such a rush to get away, I hadn't checked the friggin' gas level. Motor coughed again. Then in mid-cough, it quit.

No! I slapped the motor in frustration. Don't give up now! I pressed the starter button. Nothing.

The boat was wallowing like crazy. At the mercy of every wave. Had to get it moving forward right now. Or it'd get swamped with water and sink. Had to move fast.

A couple of heavy oars were stowed along the gunnels. As the sea bashed against the wallowing boat, I yanked the oars loose. Icy fingers trembling like mad. But I fitted the heavy metal oarlocks into their holders. One on each side of the hull. Sitting in the centre of the boat, I tried to row. Push, pull, push, pull, push . . . Tried to get both oars synchronized. But they flopped around bashing my elbow.

"Come on!" I yelled as the oars splashed water into my face. "Come on, stupid idiot. Come on. You can do it. Concentrate. Concentrate."

There. That's it. That's better. Both oars working together. The boat crept forward. Slow going but making progress. Good thing I'd had practice rowing at that camp last summer.

But oh, how my shoulders and arms ached with the effort. These oars were as heavy as a load of rocks.

The boat reached the jutting reef near the dock. Drifted behind it. Finally the wave action dropped. Closer and closer the boat coasted in to the dock. The bow bounced against the mooring float. There. At last. Safe.

Dizzy with relief, I stowed the oars back along the gunnels and shook out my aching arms and shoulders. I crawled out over the bow and tied it to the float. It swayed and bounced with each wave. But, man, compared to getting bashed around in that wild water in a boat with a dead motor, this felt like a hammock swinging in a breeze.

My legs were wobbly, my clothes were soaked and I was sweating like a sumo wrestler. But I was safe.

I pulled off the PFD and shouldered my pack. Then I took in a good deep breath and climbed the ramp, clutching the hand railing with trembling fingers. Maureen was going to be so mad at me for taking her stupid boat. I might as well face the music now and get it over with.

Chapter 19

KALU

"SHE'S GONE NOW," Kalu told Aisha. "The girl's gone. And her boat's gone too."

"Are you sure?"

Kalu pushed through the bushes hiding their cave and scanned the water in front of their bay. "Yes. But she left something beside our fire pit down there. A bag."

"What's in it, do you think?"

"I'll go down and check."

Kalu clambered down the cliff. When he got to the bottom, he waited, listening hard. A big bird flew by overhead on wings that made swishing sounds through the air. It squawked down at him, but continued flying over the cliff. He couldn't hear anything else now except the waves crashing on the rocks. He crept along the beach to the bag beside their fire pit.

"Food!" he called up to Aisha, grinning. "The girl's left some food."

He was about to climb back up the cliff to show her when he saw something else on a rock beside their fire pit. A leather pouch. When he looked inside he found a watch. A silver watch with strange numbers on its face. He looked closely at them and realized they were Roman numerals that he'd learnt about in math a couple of years ago. It was quite a large watch, bigger than the watch his teacher had worn on his wrist. He put the watch into the plastic bag with the food.

The girl had left the denim bag with his stones under the same rock. He put it into the plastic bag as well, along with their empty sardine tin. He scattered their ashes and shells so no one would suspect there'd been a fire here. Then he climbed back up the cliff to the cave to show Aisha their treasures.

"How about this bread and cheese. You should eat, you know." He coaxed Aisha.

"Not so hungry. You have it." She coughed and wiped her nose on her shirt. "Maybe I could have some of the orange though."

He peeled the orange, stashing the peel into the plastic bag for later. Then he gave her a juicy section that she nibbled slowly. He ate a couple of sections himself but gave the rest to her. "It'll be good for your cough."

"Are there any more oranges in there?" she asked, peering into the bag.

"No. That's it."

"What's this?" She pulled out the leather pouch.

"Look inside. There's a watch in there. A silver watch."

"Oh. Mister Elliot had a watch, but he wore it on his wrist," she said. "And so did Teacher."

She didn't say anything else, but she looked so sad he thought she might be about to start crying. Kalu knew she was thinking about their kind teacher and the terrible thing that had happened to him. That had happened to everyone in their village. Their whole family.

"Listen, Aisha," he said. "This watch speaks. It says, 'tick-tick-tick.'" He put the watch to her ear.

She nodded and smiled her gap-tooth smile while she listened. Then she sighed deeply and curled up under her shawl with the watch still at her ear. She sighed again and was asleep before Kalu could say anything else.

All that was left in the plastic bag now was his sardine tin, the orange peel and a water bottle half full. And his cloth bag, of course.

In it, he had three matches left but not a speck of food, and his stomach felt as hollow as ever.

While Aisha slept, he'd try his luck again at catching a nice plump fish they could roast over the fire for their supper.

And maybe Mister Elliot would be here by then.

Chapter 20

SPIKE

FROM THE RAMP, I watched Maureen leaving the lighthouse. She was following the two government guys along the trail leading down to the dock.

"Bit of a harsh day to be out there, young lady," the older one called to me. "Are you from around here?"

"That's my niece, um, Spike," Maureen told the men, frowning down at me. "Come from Canada to stay with me on the island for a while."

I raked my wet hair away from my eyes and shrugged. "Bit windy today, but really not so bad," I said in my calmest most cheerful voice.

Maureen raised her eyebrows at me, but didn't say anything else as she continued to follow Tweedle Dee and Tweedle Dumb down the path to the dock.

Something the older guy was telling Maureen made my
ears perk up.

"...just keep a watch out for some people who've been
sighted coming over from Spain, we think. Or maybe even
from northern Africa. We don't know for sure. Probably
illegal migrants. Might be refugees. Maybe travelling in fishing boats. Might be engaged in smuggling. Let us know if you
see anything suspicious or unusual out there on the water."

That fire and those footprints on the other side of the
island! Maybe that's whose they were. Illegal migrants. Or
smugglers.

Maureen waved goodbye to the men, who climbed into
their fancy sleek boat after untying it and left, bashing through
the heavy seas. Then she brought her frown up to the house
where I was sitting on the front steps, braced for her anger.

Here it comes...

"So what do you think you were doing, going out in the
boat on such a windy day?" Maureen's arms were crossed
tightly, angrily. "I told you to wait until I could take you when
the sea was calmer, so I did. You know how dangerous it is
out there? It's a wonder the boat didn't get swamped in those
waves. It's not meant for big seas like that. Where were you
off to, anyway?"

"Just puttered around. Didn't go far." I shrugged. "Not like there's a whole lot of stuff to do around here."

Maureen shut her eyes and heaved a heavy sigh. "I was worried this was no place to send a girl used to city life. Do you see that lighthouse?"

"Yeah. So?"

"That lighthouse is here for one good reason. And that reason is that the seas around here are unpredictable. They can be calm as silk one minute, then the west wind comes up and before you know it, waves start bashing the rocks. The water gets so rough even big, sea-worthy boats, never mind small runabouts like the *Sea Quest*, can easily get into trouble. And they do. Often. So unless the sea's calm as a pond, and the forecast says it's staying that way, we don't take that boat out. Understand?"

"I guess." I shrugged again.

"Come and get into some dry clothes. I'll get our tea on."

"Tea" was a replay of yesterday's tuna casserole, but at least there was a crisp salad that came out of a bag, a fresh loaf of whole-wheat bread and a pot of cream cheese.

"The government fellows were kind enough to bring me fresh provisions, even some shop-sliced bread which makes a change from my homemade brown bread," Maureen said. "Help yourself." Her tone was cold and brisk. She was still so mad she could barely stand to look at me.

I ignored her. What else could I do? Besides, I didn't really care how she felt about me. Why should I? It's not like I was sticking around this stupid place much longer.

When I bit into a crusty slice of bread smeared with cream cheese, hunger flooded my insides. Except for that orange, I hadn't eaten since breakfast and didn't realize how famished I was.

Maureen, though, had no appetite. She poked at her salad, staring out the window beside the table at dark clouds scuttling across the horizon.

"So what did the government guys say?" I asked, although I wasn't all that interested. I helped myself to a large helping of the vulture-crotch-smelling tuna casserole and tucked in. Surprisingly, it tasted not that bad.

Maureen pulled her eyes from the window. "They said they'd file a report that the lighthouse is in good shape, but they told me not to hold out too much hope I'll be able to stay on. They said keeping the lighthouse going was too big a job for a single woman to handle on her own. Like what would happen if I got sick, they wondered. For God's sake, I haven't had anything worse than a cold for these past ten years, at least."

"Why don't you pack it in? Move to the mainland. Get a job there? Wouldn't life be a lot easier?"

Maureen shook her head. "I told you, I promised Gerry I'd stay here as long as I could. Besides, an automatic system for the lighthouse just wouldn't work for this area. Somehow I just can't make them understand that. I'm sure the number of shipwrecks would increase. So would the number of lives lost. Someone needs to be right here on the island to turn on the warning horn when sudden fogs appear, or call in the coast guard when a boat's in trouble. Anyway, what would I do if I moved to the mainland?"

"Don't know. Get a regular job, I guess."

"Doing what?"

I shrugged. "Must be plenty of jobs you could do."

"No doubt. But this is where I want to spend my time, being a lighthouse keeper, as long as I'm able. Right here on Last Chance Island. This is where I belong. It's my home. It's my life. When we're finished eating, I'd like to show you something."

After tea, I pulled on a down vest and followed Maureen outside and along a trail past the lighthouse. The wind hadn't died down. If anything, it was even stronger now. Blew right through my clothes. I zipped the vest up to my chin and trailed behind, battling through the wind, as Maureen led the way through the dark shadows with a flashlight.

She stopped on the other side of the lighthouse. There, in a hollow between the path and the steep rocky cliff, were several crosses. Two white crosses were off to the side. She flashed her light on them. One was weather-worn and old with clumps of purple heather growing around it. The other was bigger and freshly painted.

"Gerry?" I guessed.

"Yes." Maureen stroked the cross. "He'll have a view of the sea for all of eternity, so he will. Exactly what he would have wanted."

"The other cross?"

"For our son, Peter. My, what a fine lad he was. Always so happy and cheerful." She smiled, remembering. Then a shadow crossed her forehead. "When he was just eight months old and starting to crawl around like a mad beetle, he caught the croup and died. Just like that. Before we could get him into Skibberoo and the clinic there. It was quick. So very quick . . ." She sighed and wiped a tear. "He would have been fifteen this summer. Same age as you. Imagine!"

I nodded, shivering with cold. I pulled the vest closer around my neck.

Now I understood why Maureen wanted to never leave Last Chance Island.

Chapter 21

KALU

AISHA'S COUGHING WOKE Kalu. She was coughing hard, shivering and moaning. The bush outside their cave did little to stop the cold wind.

"There's a little more water in the water bottle," Kalu told her. It was so dark he could barely see the bottle. He felt for it where it had rolled beside her. "Here. Drink. I put an orange peel in it so it'll taste good."

Aisha sipped the water. It helped her cough for a while but she soon started coughing again. She tried to sip more water. "It's empty now," she croaked. "No more water. My throat. It hurts."

"Maybe chew on the bit of orange peel from the bottle. It might help your throat." He shook the bottle until the small piece of soggy orange peel came out into her hand.

The wind was howling all around them. Even the branches in front of the cave entrance were blowing around, making the cave so drafty the plastic bags rustled. It sounded as if the waves below were bashing right up against their cliff. Good thing this cave was so high up. At least the sea couldn't reach them here. The rain could though. It blew into the cave in gusts. Kalu's shirt was wet. He shivered.

"Let's try to sleep, Aisha. Morning will come sooner if we do."

She was curled up under Mister Elliot's crinkly plastic bag. He spread the other one on her legs to try to keep them dry.

There was another huge crash as a wave walloped their cliff. Aisha squealed.

"It'll be OK." Kalu tried to reassure her. "The waves can't reach our cave. No matter what. We're so high up the cliff. Here, listen to the watch. That will help you sleep."

Aisha put the silver watch to her ear. "No tick-tick," she said.

He listened but he couldn't hear anything either. He shook the watch but still, it was silent.

"Maybe it's too cold," she said, slipping it back into its leather pouch.

"We'll look at it in the morning. Let's try to get to sleep now."

Kalu couldn't stretch out his legs because the bushes stopped them. If his feet were hanging over the ledge, they'd get wet in the rain and probably freeze right off.

"Maybe play your flute, Kalu? Play the 'Basa.' I like that one. That was Mama's favourite. Remember how she sang, 'Basa, basa, basa,' and danced around the fire with some of the aunties, and they all clapped their hands?"

"OK, I'll play and you can sing." Kalu sat up and pulled out his flute. He blew into it and found the tune. He didn't need the light to play the notes. His fingers knew exactly where to go.

As he played, Aisha sang and hummed along, clapping her hands softly, bouncing her knees to keep time.

When he came to the end of the tune, Aisha lay down and was quiet for a long time. He thought she was asleep until he heard her sniff.

"Do you think we'll ever see them again, Kalu? Will we see our families again?"

"I think we will," he said with more conviction than he felt. "I'm sure we'll all be together again one day." He shook his head as he remembered the searing heat from the flames as his village burnt. He knew deep down that even if they could go home, back to their village, there would be nothing left but the charred remains of everything and everyone he'd known.

Aisha sniffed louder and although it was dark, he knew she was crying.

He felt like crying too. Instead, he said, "Here's another tune for you, Aisha. This one's for when the babies are so tired all they want to do is shut their eyes and go to sleep."

After he played the soft and slow tune for a while, he heard Aisha sigh deeply and start snoring. She was finally asleep.

Now would he be able to fall asleep with all the noise of the wind and the crashing waves? He was shivering with cold. He crossed his arms, hugging what little warmth he had left and eventually he fell asleep.

The next thing he knew, it was morning. He parted the bushes and saw that the sun was rising right out of the heaving sea. The wind had dropped to nothing and the waves below were gently lapping the rocks.

He scanned the horizon hopefully. But there were no boats. Still no *Irish Queen*. And still no Mister Elliot.

His stomach grumbled. Aisha was fast asleep, snoring gently.

He clambered down the cliff. The moss had been soaked by the rain and the crashing surf in the night. It gave off a sweet spicy odour in the morning sunshine. The sun was bright and the sea was as calm as he'd ever seen it.

A perfect morning to be cruising out on the water. A perfect morning for Mister Elliot to come and get them.

"Please, please, please make Mister Elliot come soon," he prayed to the morning sun and to the blue sky. "Make him come today. Before it's too late."

Chapter 22

SPIKE

ALL NIGHT I COULD hear the wind howling around the house like a pack of lost wolves. And all night the lighthouse's revolving beam kept watch on the stormy sea. Every few seconds the beam swept my bedroom window and lit up the entire room. The thin yellow curtains didn't do much to block its glow. I burrowed into the blankets to get away from the light and eventually fell into a deep sleep.

The next morning I awoke, blinking at an even stronger light. Sunshine! I bounced up and pulled back the curtains. Couldn't believe it. Beyond the lighthouse, the sea was glassy smooth and I couldn't see a single cloud in the sky. Hard to imagine it was the same place as last night's storm.

Pulling on clean jeans and a rumpled but clean-ish t-shirt, I wondered what time it was. I rummaged through my backpack for my mother's pocket watch. Not there. Oh-oh. I searched some more, starting to get frantic now. No watch!

Heart thumping, I dumped out everything and pawed through it, shaking the sweatshirt and extra jeans. The watch *had* to be here. Just *had* to be.

But it wasn't! Where could it be? Under the bed? Just wet jeans from yesterday. I kicked them back.

Calm down, I told myself. Think! When was the last time I had the watch? Yesterday. Right. On the other side of the island. I took the watch out, I remembered, while I was eating that orange.

Oh no! I must have left it there on the rock. Stupid. Stupid. Stupid. I had to get it back. Now.

I dashed to the kitchen.

Maureen was drinking tea, working on her laptop at the table.

"Help yourself to porridge," she offered, glancing up from the screen.

Calm down now, I told myself again, carrying a bowl to the stove and staring at the pot. Friggin' porridge again. But since my churning stomach felt hollow, I'd settle for a bowl. Meanwhile, how could I get her to let me have the boat so I could get my watch? I didn't dare tell her I'd left it way over on the other side of the island. Then she'd know I'd gone that far in her boat.

With a bowl of steaming cereal buried under a thick layer of brown sugar, I sat opposite her. Pulled in a deep breath. Tried to be cool. "Doing some research?"

"Looking for a new generator I can afford," Maureen said.

"You sure need one."

"You're entirely right."

"Looks calm as a swimming pool out there this morning. OK if I take the boat out for a while?"

She started to shake her head.

"Please," I begged. "Pleeee-se."

She sighed. "Where's it you're thinking of going?"

"Not far. Thought I'd explore around the island a bit." Tried to keep my voice casual, like I was asking if I could take a walk around the block.

"You say you know about boats?"

"Sure thing. Like I told you, I've taken my father's boat out on the lake tons of times, since I was ten. And his boat's at least twice the size of your *Sea Quest*." I didn't have to tell her most of those times were without his permission. Or knowledge.

"I don't know . . ."

"I won't go far. Just want to putter around. Give me something to do."

"Well . . ." Maureen stared at me, thinking. "Maybe since it's so calm this morning, all right. But only if you promise to stay right close to shore."

"No problem."

"And return immediately if the wind comes up."

"Right."

"Take the shortwave radio and wear a life jacket," Maureen said. "And call me right away if you need help."

"OK. OK. Thanks." I'd promise anything, so long as I could use the friggin' boat. "Um, I think maybe the boat's out of gas."

"You'll find gas in the shed on the dock. Take some lunch if you want but you should really be back before noon. Usually it's in the afternoon the winds quicken."

I was going to say no thanks, but thought maybe I'd be hungry soon after the bowl of stodgy porridge. So I slapped a couple of slices of bread from last night's loaf around some cheese and grabbed an orange and a fresh banana from the fruit bowl. I filled a plastic water bottle, stuck it all into a plastic shopping bag and stuffed it into my backpack. Then headed for the door.

"See you later then, love," Maureen said, looking up from the laptop screen. "And please, do be careful."

I was soon on my way, puttering along in the small boat, after putting some gas in its tank. The sea was so peaceful and flat, it mirrored the moss and dry grasses on the island's rocky cliffs. Perfect day to head to the mainland and hop the train to Dublin, but I had to find my mother's watch first. If it wasn't on the other side of the island, I just didn't know what I'd do.

In the quiet water, it didn't take long to reach the small

inlet. I recognized the sharp pillar of rock that jutted up from the cliff and steered the boat close to the rocky beach. I turned off the motor and swung it up out of the water. The boat's hull crunched onto the rocks and slid to a stop. After pulling off my shoes, I splashed to shore. This time I threw the boat's rope around a rock and tied it. Didn't want a repeat of yesterday's boat drifting away.

In the sparkling sunshine, the beach looked so different from yesterday, at first I wasn't sure it was the same one. But there was the pillar rock and the faint trail leading through the scrubby bushes to the cliff.

I hurried to the rock where I'd seen the remains of a fire, but there was no sign anyone had been there lately. And no sign of my mother's watch in its leather pouch. Even the food bag was gone. Tears sprang to my eyes. I was so sure I'd left the watch right here. Maybe I was mistaken.

But, no. There were the few charred bits of wood from the campfire. Looked pretty much the same as yesterday, although the ashes looked more scattered, probably by the wind. I lifted the flat rock beside the fire pit. No denim bag. Sardine can was gone as well.

Maybe I'd imagined the whole thing? Or maybe the wind had blown the leather pouch and food bag into a crevice? I grabbed a stick and poked around between the rocks. Nothing. Scoured the surrounding rocks. Still nothing. Not even a scrap of garbage. Maybe someone had found the watch and taken it, along with the denim pouch. That must be it! Now my heart was really pounding. I *had* to find that watch.

Should I call out? But if someone was close by, he or she must know I was here because he'd have heard the boat's motor.

I hunkered down on a ledge beside the rocky cliff and leaned back to think. In this protected spot out of the breeze, the weak rays of the sun were actually warm. I pulled in a deep breath. Smelled nice here. Sort of spicy.

I concentrated really hard, going over every second I'd spent here yesterday.

I'd had that watch forever. If I'd lost it, I didn't know what I'd do. I was so totally, totally alone now without even the tick of my mother's watch for company. No Mom. No Dad. No family . . .

"Get a grip," I muttered to myself. "It's just a stupid watch."

But my insides ached.

Stretching out one of my legs, I remembered the street musicians in Dublin and Kieran O'Grady's friendly invitation. Maybe I'll just forget the watch and head over to the mainland after all. The water was invitingly peaceful and serene, and the foothills were visible in the hazy distance. Even in that small boat, I could probably make it there in an hour or two on such a calm day.

But could I go without my mother's watch?

Besides, I probably didn't have enough fuel in the tank to reach the shore. I should have thought of that and brought along an extra can. Maybe tomorrow, I'll venture out, if the weather holds . . .

Planning my escape and how I'd find my new friends in Dublin, I leaned back onto the cliff face again.

Then I heard it. Voices! Whispering!

I held my breath and listened hard. My leg was cramping under me but I forced myself to stay still. Maybe it was just the wind. Or maybe the chatter of squirrels or chipmunks?

No. There it was again. People chatter. Or maybe the Selkies. Did they talk? Is that how they sounded?

Where was the whispering coming from? Cliff above me?

I stared up at the cliff. I was absolutely certain it was people talking.

Chapter 23

KALU

"AISHA. THE GIRL. She's back," Kalu whispered, nudging his cousin's arm.

Aisha woke from her doze. She was feeling worse today and her nose was running even more now. She rubbed her eyes and blinked. She stared past the bushes in front of their cave. Down at the water's edge, the girl was splashing from a small boat to the beach.

There she was, raking her fingers through her strange purple hair and looking all around. She was checking out their fire pit again, poking at it with a stick. Although Kalu had swept it pretty clean of any evidence of their fire and had removed the shellfish shells and the sardine tin, she still seemed interested in it.

Aisha held the leather pouch close to her chest.

"The clock inside still isn't ticking. Maybe the girl can fix it. Maybe she knows how."

"But we can't take a chance, Aisha. If she sees us, she'll report us to the coast guard or the police, and they'll come and get us and throw us in jail. Remember what Mister Elliot said."

Aisha's eyes grew big with fear. "But what if Mister Elliot never comes back for us? What will we do then?"

"He'll come back. He said he would."

"But we have nothing left to eat or drink now."

"Maybe the girl will leave some food behind like she did yesterday." Kalu's stomach grumbled as he remembered that delicious juicy orange he'd shared with his cousin.

Aisha shook the silver watch and held it to her ear. "Still no tick-tick."

"Sh-sh." Kalu put his finger to his lips. "Look. The girl. Now she's poking around the cliffs. She's calling out. Maybe she knows we're here . . ."

Aisha pushed aside the bush in front of the cave to get a better look.

"Don't," Kalu hissed. "She might see us."

Aisha pulled back into the cave. She sniffed, wiping her nose on the edge of her shawl. "I'm thirsty, Kalu. So thirsty. And my throat. It's so sore." She sniffed again.

"When the girl leaves I'll try to find some fresh water for you. Maybe there's a puddle left from last night's rain." He put his finger at his mouth. "Shh. Be very quiet now."

The girl was looking around the cliff. Now she was calling out again. Louder this time. She was staring up right at their cave.

Kalu held his breath and prayed that Aisha wouldn't cough.

Chapter 24

SPIKE

I WAS SURE I'D HEARD voices up there. But that was straight up a cliff way too steep to climb. If it was Selkies, maybe they were sort of magic and could climb sheer cliffs. Or maybe there was an easier way up somewhere else.

I scrambled along the bottom of the rocky cliff searching for a possible route.

"Hello!" I called out. "Anyone there? Anyone?"

No answer. Of course.

I couldn't see any path up the stone cliff so I retraced my steps thinking about the fact the food I'd left behind yesterday was gone. That didn't prove someone was here. It could have blown away. Or maybe some animal had taken it. Big bird of prey? Hawk or eagle? Or one of those noisy seagulls, more likely. Also, the denim pouch I'd left under the rock was gone. And so was my mother's watch.

I shouted again, "Hello! Anyone there?" Then added, "I come in peace. Peace," I said louder, holding out my fingers in a peace sign.

Still no answer. I searched the steep cliff one last time. Then shrugging, I gave up. I splashed back to the boat and climbed in. As I reached over my shoulder to put the key into the motor, I saw my backpack under the seat. An idea popped into my head.

I pulled out the food bag, went back up the beach to a bunch of shrubs and tied it to the tallest branch. After taking another good look around, I made a big show of climbing back into the boat and leaving, like I was heading back to the lighthouse.

But when the boat was past the bend of land, I shut off the motor and pushed the boat into some shrubs near the water's edge. After tying the boat to an overhanging branch, I got out, leaving my shoes on this time, and quietly waded through the thigh-deep water. Man, was it freezing.

I crept back along the edge of the beach not daring to make a splash. I ducked behind some rocks on shore where I could see the plastic lunch bag fluttering in the light breeze. I waited.

Not for long. Soon I heard the sound of footsteps running

lightly along the path I'd taken earlier. Wow! My bait was working.

I ducked lower behind the rock as the footsteps came closer. And closer. Footsteps stopped. All was silent. Not even a bit of wind stirred the twigs. It was like the world was holding its breath.

I peeked over the rock but didn't see anyone. Then the soft footsteps again. Sneaking even closer. And closer.

Still keeping out of sight, I silently eased myself forward. I heard the bag flutter and I erupted out of the bushes.

A boy! Dressed in a ragged shirt and shorts. Green woolly hat pulled over his hair. And a brown face!

"Hey!" I yelled. "You!"

The boy dropped the bag and dashed away.

I raced after him. "Hey! Don't run away. I won't hurt you!"

But he glanced back over his shoulder, eyes huge with fear, and kept running, bounding over rocks and branches like a terrified deer.

"Stop! Stop!" I shouted. "If you need food, you can have it. Have it all."

He veered sharply. Started scuttling up the cliff, grabbing onto cracks in the rock and fern roots. Agile as a monkey, climbing straight up, green hat bobbing.

I sprinted back, scooped up the lunch bag and dashed to the cliff. Scrambled up, trying to follow the boy. Tough going. Then I found a slanting crack in the cliff, barely wide enough to balance on my toes. I pulled the bag over one shoulder and reached for a root to haul myself higher up the cliff. Cautiously, I scaled the steep rock face, and finally came to a ledge wide enough for my whole foot.

Now what? Where was he? What direction had the kid gone?

He'd just friggin' vanished. Like, *poof*.

The ledge going right looked a bit wider and more worn so I followed it. Shunting myself along, clinging onto the cliff.

A hacking cough, soon stifled! I held my breath, listening hard. That cough was close. Very close.

I eased forward along the ledge, heading to some scrubby bushes growing from a crack in the rock. Shuffling sound, right above me. I glanced up.

The boy! Crouched on a higher ledge. Staring down at me.

I pulled back in surprise. "Who are you? What are you doing here?"

He stared down at me with huge scared eyes. Tucked into the waist of his ragged shorts was a thin wooden rod. Maybe the flute I'd heard the last couple days?

"I won't hurt you. Look." I pushed back my hair and held out the plastic bag. "Brought you food. Something to eat."

He still didn't say anything.

"Food," I repeated. "For you. To eat. Good. You want it?"

He stared longingly at the bag, licking his lips. I could tell his mouth was watering. Instead of asking for food, he said, "Medicine. I need medicine. Now." His voice was high and his accent was sing-songy.

"Medicine? What sort of medicine?"

He shrugged. "For cold, fever."

"You don't have a fever, do you?" I squinted up at him. Looked healthy enough, although he was probably the skinniest person I'd ever seen. Brown legs sticking out from the ragged shorts were thinner than my arm and his dusty knees and elbows were pointy.

Then I heard the hacking cough I'd heard earlier. But it was closer. Just to my right. I eased along the narrow ledge to the bushes.

The boy clambered frantically down the cliff toward me. But before he reached me, I pushed back the bushes. A cave!

Two eyes stared out at me. Two scared eyes.

A little kid cringed away in the shadows.

"Who are you? Where'd you come from? How did you get here?" A thousand other questions crashed around in my head. But I stopped asking when the little girl coughed again and again, each deep cough wrenching her thin chest as she put her hand up to her mouth to try to stifle the sound. But it was a terrible cough. Sounded as if she was about to cough up her insides.

"Don't worry. I won't hurt you." I fumbled open the lunch bag. "Here's some food. An orange? Some water?" I didn't know if she understood English. I pushed through the scrubby branches and knelt in the dirt beside her in the cave. Screwed off the water bottle cap and tried to push it into her reluctant hands. "Drink, drink, kiddo. Water. It's good. Good."

Rustling behind me. I pulled aside the scrub and saw the thin boy approaching on the ledge. He pushed into the cave in front of the cringing kid, fists clenched. Ready to fight to protect her.

"Don't worry, dude. I'm not going to hurt her. Or you. I'm just giving her some water. Water?" I tried again to push the bottle into the little girl's hands.

The girl looked up at the boy with those huge scared eyes. He lowered his fists and nodded slightly so she took the bottle and sipped. Then she sighed and shutting her feverish eyes, she lay back on a scrap of clothing and moss.

I didn't know much about sick people but this girl with her glittering eyes and runny nose didn't look at all healthy. And that cough sounded terrible.

"So it's your sister you need the medicine for," I said to the boy. "Why didn't you say so?"

"Food?" He ignored my question and stared at my lunch bag. "You have food?"

"I have food." I clasped the bag under my elbow. "Before I give it to you, you have to tell me what you and your sister are doing here. Where d'you come from? How did you get here? Who brought you? How long have you been here?"

"Too many questions." He shook his head. "Too many."

"OK. What's your name then?"

"Name? Um, I'm Kalu. My cousin, she is called Aisha."

"So Kalu and Aisha. Just tell me where you came from, and I'll give you this scrumptious cheese sandwich." I held the sandwich out enticingly near the boy's face.

Staring at the sandwich, he swallowed hard, shaking his head. Finally he said, "You must tell no one."

"OK, dude. I won't tell anyone. Promise." I patted my chest. "So where d'you come from?"

"Um." He stared at me for a minute then nodded, making up his mind. "From a fisherman. A fisherman take us here. He say we can't go closer to land. They find us and we have to go back. Too much danger. For him also."

"Who? Take you back where?" I asked, taunting the boy with the sandwich.

But he just shrugged and wouldn't say anything else.

"OK, here's the food." I finally gave it to him.

He broke off a small piece that he pushed into his mouth and chewed eagerly while giving the larger portion to the girl, coaxing her to open her mouth and eat.

I couldn't stand it. He was probably the skinniest, hungriest person I'd ever seen in my entire life, and here he was, giving away most of the sandwich to his cousin. I pulled out the other sandwich and thrust it at him. "Take it. Eat."

He smiled at me, flashing white teeth and bowed his head, thanks. He bit into the bread, and closing his eyes, devoured the whole thing, wiping his mouth on the back of his hand.

Meanwhile the little girl had hardly touched her portion. He nodded to her to eat, but she shook her head and started that awful coughing again. When it was over, she curled up onto the rags again with her eyes closed.

"Medicine," the boy said to me. "You get medicine for my cousin, yes?"

"I think your cousin needs a lot more than friggin' medicine, dude. She needs a warm bed and some good chicken soup. And probably a good hot bath wouldn't hurt. That cough sounds so bad. How about I take you both back to the lighthouse on the boat and my aunt will look after her?"

"No, we must remain here."

"Here in this cave?"

He nodded.

"But why?"

"The fisherman. He comes back for us, he says."

"When did he say that? How long since you've seen him?"

"Four, five days, maybe." Kalu shrugged. "Don't know for sure."

"Look. Could be he won't be coming back at all. Ever. Have you thought of that? Could be he just dumped you here. Maybe he had a change of plans. Like maybe he had to go somewhere else. Or . . ."

Again, Aisha's hacking cough interrupted. She coughed and coughed. It was hard to believe that such a deep hacking cough could come from such a skinny little kid. When she was finished coughing, she collapsed back onto her rags before I could coax her to drink more water. A cold breeze blew up from the sea.

I turned to Kalu. "Really, dude. We've got to get help for your cousin. Right now. Don't you see if we just leave her here in this cold cave, she could die? She's really sick, and she might not make it through one more night."

But still he shook his head, his brow scrunched up with worry.

"OK, how about this then? How about I take her in the boat to the lighthouse for my aunt to look after her? And you can wait here for your fisherman friend. Who, by the way, probably won't ever be coming back."

Kalu whispered to his cousin in a different language. I couldn't understand what he was saying. But she opened her eyes and shook her head, even more scared.

"She is too afraid to go anywhere without me."

"Well, that settles it, doesn't it? You'll just have to come, too. Honestly, it looks like a matter of life and death. Your little cousin's life. You see that, don't you? It's all up to you."

He shook his head. "But . . ."

That's when I saw it! There, among the girl's rags.

"My mother's watch!" I grabbed the pouch.

The kids pulled back as if I'd punched them both in the face.

"You found my mother's watch," I told them laughing. "I was searching all over for it."

"That bag is your mother's?"

I nodded. "Left it on the rocks yesterday. See." I shook the watch out of the pouch. "I was so worried I'd never find it."

"Aisha say the tick-tick, it stopped."

"Here, let me wind it up, then you can hear it tick."

I wound it and held it to the boy's ear. He grinned. Then I held it to the little girl's ear. It had the strangest effect on her. She didn't smile or anything, but she took a deep breath and stopped looking so scared and agitated. The sound calmed her right down. But she started coughing again so I slipped the watch back into its pouch and pulled it around my neck.

"Now," I told them in my most business-like voice. "I'm going down to get the boat. And I'll bring it up the beach as far as I can so you can get in. OK?"

"But, but . . ." Kalu protested.

Before he had time to say anything else, I slid down the cliff and hurried back along the beach through the underbrush to where I'd tied up the boat. "Oh, he'd better come," I muttered to myself, holding my watch close against my chest. "He's just got to."

Chapter 25

KALU

"AISHA. WE MUST GO with the girl now. We have to trust her. You see that, don't you?"

"But what about Mister Elliot? What if he comes and we're not here?"

Kalu didn't say anything for a few minutes. "Maybe the girl is right. Maybe he won't be coming back for us after all." He hadn't wanted to tell her that for the last day or so, he had been suspecting Mister Elliot had forgotten about them.

He saw his cousin was still scared to go. But the girl might be their one chance to get to safety. And also, he knew Aisha needed help. She was getting sicker. She needed medicine and food, and a warm place to get better.

Besides, there was something about the tall girl that made him trust her. Something about her eyes, maybe. The way she stared right at you. Only someone who told the truth could look at you so directly, so intently . . .

"Look. I promise I'll stay right beside you the whole time. Every minute. And if anything happens that we don't like, we can run away. It's not like we'll be locked up in a prison."

Aisha started coughing, and he gave her the girl's water bottle. She took a sip and that seemed to help.

"The girl will have medicine for you. Medicine to make that cough all better. And probably somewhere warm where we can stay."

"All right," Aisha said. "If you promise to stay right with me the whole time."

"I promise."

He checked that he had his bamboo flute tucked securely into his belt. And that the denim bag with the rocks from home was in his pocket.

Aisha tied the ragged shawl around her shoulders and stood up on shaky legs. "Let's go."

He helped her start climbing down the cliff. A cold breeze caught his back, and Aisha's too. He saw her shiver. She hesitated.

"We can do it, Aisha. It's not far down. The girl will be waiting for us with her boat. Here. Let me help you down this bit . . ."

Chapter 26

SPIKE

WAVES HAD PUSHED the small boat sideways, right into bushes overhanging the water, so I had to slog through the freezing thigh-deep water to pull it clear before I could get in. Finally it was free. I sat in the stern, lowered the motor and put in the key and pressed the starter.

Soon I was back at the beach near the kids' cave. There they were, struggling down the rocky cliff, Kalu helping his young cousin, almost carrying her, wrapped in a ragged cloth. With their thin legs and arms, they looked like a couple of spiders as they crept cautiously downwards.

I leapt out of the boat to help. Together, Kalu and I helped the sick kid through the shallow water and laid her gently in the centre of the boat, her head on the PFD. She shut her eyes, shivering like crazy. I pulled off my jacket and tucked it around her small frame. Her bones felt as fragile as a baby bird's.

"Sit up front, Kalu. Keep an eye on your cousin." I pushed the boat into deeper water, climbed into the stern and started up the motor. As we coasted out of the narrow inlet, waves bounced against the hull causing it to lurch. Kalu held onto the front gunnels with both fists.

"It'll be OK, dude," I called out to reassure him. "The end of the headland catches the wind so it's usually rough here. Once we get past those rocks up ahead and back into the lee of the island, it'll get better."

I tried to steer the boat so the waves hit the hull on the quarter. That way it wouldn't rock as much, but it was tough. Blasted wind had come up and the waves were getting bigger every second.

A round grey head popped up beside the boat. And another. Two seals stared at us with shiny eyes. They sure didn't mind getting bounced around by the waves.

Or maybe they were waiting for the boat to sink. Then they'd grab us and drag us down into the depths to drown.

I turned away from their hypnotic gaze and concentrated on steering the boat around the whitecaps.

Eventually we rounded another jutting cliff and came within sight of the lighthouse's sweeping beam. Then I saw it.

The big red launch with flags fluttering. Green, white and orange.

"Oh crap!" I stamped my heel. "It's those darn government guys. Wonder why they're back?"

"We cannot go there," Kalu said. "We cannot let the government men catch us."

I remembered one of the men telling Maureen about people who may be coming over from Spain or even Africa. How she should be on the lookout for them. Illegal migrants, he'd called them. So I agreed with Kalu. He and his cousin would be in danger if those men discovered them. They'd cart the kids off somewhere. And probably somewhere not very pleasant.

Thinking fast, I pulled on the tiller, turning the boat sharply toward the island. But steep cliffs came right down to the water so there wasn't even an inch of flat rock where we could land.

"No room for the boat here," I told him. "We'll have to go back."

He nodded and I steered the boat back along the edge of the island until I spotted a tiny pocket beach between two steep cliffs.

"Think I can land over here. You and Aisha could wait on that ledge until the government guys leave and I come back for you."

Kalu stared at the narrow opening between the crashing waves and nodded again. So I steered into it until the bow scraped lightly against the rocks and I shut off the motor.

Kalu climbed out over the bow. Then pulling on the rope, he dragged the boat further up the rocks. We carefully lifted Aisha and carried her to a mossy ledge where we laid her down. She sighed and curled up like a kitten. I tucked my jacket around her thin shoulders again.

"This isn't much of a place for you two to wait. Not very comfortable."

Kalu shrugged and squatted beside his cousin. "It's OK."

I hesitated. When the tide came in, this ledge might be under water. "Maybe I should wait with you until those men leave. Just in case. You know . . ."

"No. Better you get medicine for my cousin now. Maybe more food?"

"You're right. They'll probably be leaving soon anyway. Then I'll have a chance to tell my aunt about you. OK, I'll be back as soon as I can." I patted Aisha's shivering shoulder. "One good thing. No one would guess in a million years anyone could fit between these cliffs."

I waded back through the chilly water to the boat. Shivering with wet feet and soaked jeans and without my jacket, I was on my way again, battling waves that were growing bigger with every second.

Chapter 27

KALU

NO SOONER HAD THE girl left in the boat when Kalu saw something splashing just beyond the waves. A dark body curved out of the water and then back in. And there was another one. A round head popped up and so did another. And another. Three big seals and a smaller one. They stared at him as they swam closer. They seemed to be inspecting him and Aisha.

"Aisha," he whispered. "Look. Seals. They've come to see us."

Aisha sat up and stared back at them.

The smallest seal seemed especially brave. It played around

in the frothy surf, diving and bouncing in the waves. One really big wave pushed him closer to the cliffs. He barked and wiggled his body and twitched his whiskers at them. When he dived, Kalu could see small grey patches on his dark brown back. His head popped up out of the water again and he seemed to be laughing at them.

The other seals stayed out in deeper water, barking at the smaller one. Maybe they were telling him to come back where he would be safer. But he wasn't listening.

Another big wave pushed him even closer to Kalu's bare toes. The seal was so close now that when he barked, Kalu could smell his fishy breath and see his pointy white teeth.

Kalu pulled away and scrambled up a bit higher on the cliff. He didn't want the little seal to mistake his bare toes for tasty bits of fish.

Aisha coughed and coughed. The seal barked at her and she coughed again. It was as if they were having a conversation.

Then the surging waves pulled him back out to where the bigger seals were watching. They barked a welcome. In an instant, they all dived and Kalu couldn't see them anymore.

"Goodbye, little seal," Aisha sighed. "Kalu, when do you think the girl will come back for us?"

"She should be here soon. She said she'd return for us after those men in the big boat leave."

"But what if she never comes back for us, ever? Like Mister Elliot."

For a minute Kalu didn't know what to say. It was true Mister Elliot had not come back to pick them up yet, but he probably had a good reason for that. And maybe he was on his way to get them this very minute. He stared out at the water, way into the far horizon. There wasn't a single boat out there as far as he could see.

"I am sure the girl will be here soon." He patted Aisha's leg, trying not to shiver too much, but that wind sure was cold. He pulled his woolly hat down further over his ears. At least his head was warm.

Chapter 28

SPIKE

"THERE YOU ARE! Finally," Maureen called as I steered the boat to the mooring float behind the big red boat that belonged to the Commissioners of Irish Lights. She was coming down the ramp with the same two men that were here yesterday. Tweedle Dee and Tweedle Dumb.

I threw Tweedle Dumb the rope and he tied it up as I scrambled out. "Are you waiting for me?"

"Your aunt was getting worried about you so we were about to organize a search party for you around the island," Tweedle Dee said.

"I was wondering what happened. You've been gone so long," Maureen said. "And look at you. You don't even have a jacket. You must be freezing. You'll catch your death, so you will."

"It's not all that cold." I tried not to shiver.

I was reeling at the thought of what would have happened if I hadn't let the kids off on that cliff edge. I would have delivered them right into the arms of these government guys who probably would have whisked them off to a detention centre somewhere. Or whatever they did with "illegal migrants."

"Here I am." I kept my voice cheerful. "Safe and sound. Starving too. When's supper?"

"That's another reason I wanted to find you. I managed to catch Thomas and Sloan on their way back from Jars Island and they're giving me a ride in their boat into town so I can get the new generator."

"Looks like that old one's about to give up the ghost," Tweedle Dee said.

"Right," Maureen said. "I had trouble getting it started this morning so it's time to buy a new one. But we have to leave now to get there before the shops shut. I was thinking of staying the night with my friend, Joan. She has room for you as well, of course."

"But, but . . ." My mind raced. Here was my chance! Escaping from the village and hightailing it to Dublin would be so much easier than trying to motor across the bay in Maureen's small boat on my own.

But what about the kids?

I couldn't just leave them on the edge of that tiny beach. With that steep cliff behind them, there's no way they could escape the rising tide. If I didn't pick them up soon, they'd be swept out to sea. What a thought!

Also, Aisha needed care right now. Medical care and a warm bed. But I couldn't tell Maureen about the kids. The government guys were right here. They'd overhear.

"But how would we get back to the island?" I asked Maureen, stalling for time. "And what about the light in the lighthouse? Don't you need to be here to tend it? What if that old generator fails again and can't power the light? Don't you need someone to switch it over to emergency power?"

Maureen laughed. "Here, I thought you'd leap at the chance to get off the island for a night. I've put the lamp on automatic and plugged in the foghorn so everything should be all right until tomorrow morning anyway. The generator is old and worn, but I've fixed the leads so it'll last one more night. And we can catch a ride back to the island early tomorrow morning with Seamus's taxi. No problem."

I shook my head. I couldn't go. I just couldn't. "I'll stay here. Watch the lamp for you. Make sure that old generator keeps working."

"What? But aren't you dying to get to the mainland, do some shopping? I thought we could even go out for pizza in the village tonight. Special treat."

"Naw." I tried to act cool. I raked my hair back with my fingers. "Don't really feel like pizza. Actually, I'm pretty tired. Exhausted more like." I yawned as wide as I could. "Must be the friggin' jet lag finally caught up with me." I started up the ramp to the dock.

"But, Spike . . ." Maureen called to my back.

I kept walking away from her, shaking my head. The one thing I wanted more than anything was for those government guys to just leave. Like right now. The sooner, the better. So I could get to those kids before the tide did.

"I'll be right back," Maureen called out to the men who were climbing impatiently into their boat. She followed me up the ramp. "Spike, hold on a second."

I stopped and waited for her to catch up.

"I really have to go now. Thomas and Sloan are waiting, but I can't leave you here on the island on your own. You see that, don't you?"

"I'll be OK. Really. It's just until morning, right? And like I said, I can keep an eye on things here while you're gone." Should I tell her about the kids? No, I couldn't. Not with the government guys right there. Everything would get so complicated.

"Maureen," Tweedle Dee called. "We should be heading out now. They're predicting thick fog tonight so we want to get back to town before it gets too bad."

"Hold on. I'll be right there."

"Go." I nudged her away. "Like I said, I'll be fine. I'll just have a sandwich or something for supper and watch TV. Don't worry. I'm used to staying on my own. Been doing it since I was six."

Maureen made a face and sighed. "If you're sure you can manage . . ."

"'Course, I'm sure. Positive, in fact. Go now. See you in the morning. Or whenever." I forced myself to smile at her.

"If you need me for anything, just call me on the phone in the kitchen. Joan's last name is Fagan and her number is in the phone directory right beside the phone. Or just press redial and that will take you right to Joan's. As I said, call me if you need anything. Anything at all."

"Sure, sure." I flicked my hair back and stuck my hands in my jeans pockets.

"There's some good soup leftover from lunch in the fridge," Maureen went on. "You could warm that up for your tea."

"Like I said, don't worry about me. I'll be fine." Would this woman never friggin' leave?

She gave me a quick squishy hug then hurried back down the ramp and climbed aboard the cruiser. I waved goodbye as the boat pulled away from the dock. Soon it was ploughing through the waves, bow pointing south to head around the island and back to the mainland.

I watched until it motored past the headland and was out of sight. Finally, they were gone. Yay! I hugged myself with relief.

I decided to wait a few minutes to be sure they didn't return. Then I'd head back to pick up the kids. First though, I'd grab some dry clothes and a blanket and stuff them into a plastic garbage bag.

Chapter 29

KALU

THE TIDE WAS RISING. Kalu saw that the waves crashing over the rocks were rolling in closer and closer to his feet.

"You'll have to move higher up the rock to stay dry," he told Aisha. "The water is getting deeper."

Aisha was crouched on the moss under the girl's jacket. She heaved herself up and pulled the jacket tighter around her back. When she tried to climb up the rock, the jacket fell off.

"I'll hold the coat for you until you're higher," Kalu said.

But the cliff was too steep and slippery and there was nothing but flimsy moss to hang onto. She couldn't climb much higher.

A wave crashed on the rocks and cold water surged over Kalu's feet. They'd have to hurry to escape the oncoming tide.

"Maybe I can climb up there and pull you higher." He scrambled up the slippery moss, digging his toes and fingers into tiny crevasses, pulling himself past Aisha to some ferns that had taken root in a shallow hole in the rock. "Now, Aisha. Give me your hand."

He tried to haul her up beside him. But he lost his footing and tumbled down into the foaming waves, taking her with him. She squealed.

"So sorry." He lifted her out of the water. Now they were both soaked and so was the girl's jacket.

Aisha whimpered, trembling hard. She was wet and cold and the icy waves were licking at her toes.

"I'll try pushing you up," Kalu said. "Maybe that would work better. But we'll have to hurry because the waves are getting bigger."

Aisha took in a deep breath to try to stop trembling so much. Then she strained with all her strength to scramble up the rocky cliff. Kalu pushed her up as far as he could reach. Then he climbed a foot or so up the rock and pushed her a bit higher.

"See that clump of ferns up there? Can you reach them? Good. Now pull yourself up beside them."

Aisha wound her fingers around the ferns' roots and clung to them. She crouched there, trembling even harder now, with cold and with fear.

Meanwhile, Kalu was standing below in water rising up to

his ankles. It was so cold his feet throbbed with pain. He kept moving them up and down so they wouldn't freeze. He hummed a song to keep the rhythm of his marching feet.

If the girl didn't return soon, and the tide continued to rise, he didn't know what they'd do. He couldn't climb any further up the cliff. Maybe she wouldn't be coming back for them after all.

No, he told himself. She had given her word. Still. They didn't really know her. Could she be trusted?

He was about to give up hope when he heard a boat.

Yes!

But it was not the girl's boat. It was much bigger with a much louder motor. It sprayed out a high column of water behind as it cruised past them then away from the island, causing a wake that soon came crashing even higher on the rocks. As the swelling waves tugged at Kalu's legs, he clung tightly to the cliff.

Aisha squealed.

Kalu pressed his body against the cliff and held his breath until the swells subsided.

"That must be the government men," he told Aisha, trying to keep his voice calm. "They're leaving the island. The girl will be coming for us soon."

A thick mist was swirling around the island now.

When the girl did come back, maybe she wouldn't see them. Maybe she wouldn't remember where they were. How could he tell her?

With fingers trembling from the cold, he tried to rip a strip off the hem of his shirt but couldn't. So he pulled it off over his head. It was wet anyway. The cold wind slapped against his bare back. Shivering, he tied the shirt to a bush growing out of a crack in the cliff.

Aisha was up on her perch, whimpering quietly.

"It'll be all right, Aisha. Soon the girl will be back for us," he told her again. "You'll see."

Aisha nodded but she couldn't stop crying. She was so cold and so scared. Every time a big wave rolled toward the cliff and crashed against it, she squealed again and cringed away from its icy spray.

Kalu's elbow brushed against the flute at his waist. He pulled it out and blew into it, clearing away the dampness. "Remember, Aisha, at home at the end of the day? When everyone was around the fire? We'd sing this song together? 'Kosi Baba' . . . One of your favourites, right?"

He blew into his flute again until he found the tune. Then he played and played until they were both transported away from the pounding surf and freezing mist to the warmth of their family, all resting around the evening fire, sitting close together on the warm brown Mother Earth of home.

Chapter 30

SPIKE

WEARING MY WARMEST fleece jacket and dry jeans, I was back in the boat and heading along the island's edge. I'd stuffed an extra hoodie and the puffy duvet I'd grabbed from my bed into a plastic garbage bag and stuck it under the front seat.

Had to hurry. Tide was rising, and fast. It'd be a race. What would reach the kids first? The tide or me? Or the fog? The fog the Commissioner guy had mentioned was already swirling in around the island, growing thicker.

After a while, I slowed the boat down and crept along the ferns and seaweed at the edge of the island, trying to keep out of the waves bouncing back off the steep banks. Where were the kids? I should have left some kind of marker for their hiding spot. The boat rounded the curve of land where jagged cliffs rose up out of sight, lost already in the thick swirling mist.

"Kalu! Where are you? Kalu!" My voice echoed off the cliffs.

No answer.

Maybe I hadn't gone far enough yet. The boat crept along, the motor turned so low it was barely on. The tide had definitely risen in the short time I was away. I scanned the cliffs. They were growing darker and more indistinct by the minute.

Then I saw it. A rag fluttering against the dark moss.

"Here, Missy! We are here!" Kalu. Still above the rising tide. Thank God!

Pulling the tiller, I made straight for his waving flag.

The sea had risen over the mossy mound and Kalu was standing thigh-deep in water without his shirt on. The warning flag was his shirt. God! He must be freezing! But he grinned at me, waving both arms. His cousin was propped up on a higher ledge where she was curled into a ball under my jacket and clinging to a bit of fern. At least she was out of the water.

I shut off the motor and threw Kalu the rope. He towed the boat's bow right up against the mound, but the oncoming waves hit the stern making the boat bounce around like an impatient horse.

"Hold the boat steady so I can get out," I shouted to him. I rolled up my jeans and climbed over the bow onto the flooded mound, soaking my shoes again. "The men are gone now. And my aunt went with them."

He nodded. "Good."

"Can you hold the boat right here while I get Aisha?"

"Yes." He nodded again.

I sloshed through thigh-deep water to the cliff. Freezing cold! "Come," I told her. "We're going back into the boat now."

A big wave crashed against the boat causing it to bounce wildly again. Kalu fought to hold on. Aisha pulled away from me, shaking her head, her eyes huge. She was terrified.

"You have to come, Aisha. It's just a short ride in the boat and we'll be there..." I reached up for her but again she pulled away. The boat bouncing in the surf and all the waves crashing around must be freaking her out.

My mother's watch pouch slipped out of my shirt. She eyed the pouch. I remembered how it had calmed her earlier. I pulled it over my head and slipping it around her neck, I shook out the watch and held it to her ear.

"Hear it? The tick, tick, tick? Now just listen to it. Don't think about anything else..."

"Tick, tick," she whispered, pulling in a calming breath and closing her eyes.

"You can listen to it in the boat. Come, I'll carry you there. Everything will be fine," I whispered, and lifted the kid from her ledge as gently as a fragile package. She clung to my shoulders with trembling fingers. "Soon, you'll be all nice and warm. And I'll make you some good hot soup too. Soon, soon we'll be there," I murmured to keep her calm as I carried her through the waves crashing around the boat. She felt as light as a bundle of dry kindling for a fire.

"Hold the boat as steady as you can," I told Kalu. "I'll put Aisha right there in the middle on the floor." I lifted her over the bow and climbed awkwardly into the rocking boat. I set her down and gave her the PFD for her head. I pulled the blanket out of the garbage bag to tuck around her, and she curled up with the watch still at her ear.

I scrambled to the stern. In spite of my fleecy jacket, I was shivering like mad since my shoes and jeans were soaked through. But Kalu must be a lot colder. He didn't even have a shirt on. And that wind was something else.

"OK, dude. Give us a big push off then jump in."

After he clambered into the boat over the bow I told him a hoodie was in the bag under the front seat for him. He pulled it over his head and nodded his thanks. The hoodie was enormous on him. Made him look like a rapper. It should help cut the wind.

When I pressed the starter, the motor coughed before firing, but it caught and we were on our way to the lighthouse. Again, I tried to keep the boat close to the island's edge, following its curve around cliffs and reefs, but the swirling fog was so thick now, I could barely see them.

"Watch for rocks in the water, OK, dude?" I called, slowing the boat down to a crawl. Kalu nodded from his perch on the front seat and stared out at the waves.

Before we'd gone far, the motor coughed again. Then it stalled.

A feeling of dread filled my stomach. I pressed the starter button but nothing happened. The boat wallowed around in the waves.

Kalu looked back at me, eyebrows raised, worried.

"Darn!" I said. "Forgot to put in more gas. We've probably friggin' run out."

"Now what to do?"

"We'll have to row. Can't be that far to the dock." I unhitched the heavy wooden oars from the sides of the boat and fitted them into the oarlocks.

"Should I row?" he offered.

"No, I've done it before. But we'll have to move Aisha because I'll have to sit on the middle seat there."

So together we shifted the little kid into the stern beside the motor. She was wrapped in the blanket with the watch still at her ear. Her eyes were closed and she was breathing shallowly. Asleep, I thought. Or unconscious.

I started rowing, dipping the oars into the waves and pulling back on them.

"Tell me if we're heading in the right direction," I told Kalu, trying to get the oars to row symmetrically. "And keep watching for rocks."

It took awhile to get the boat moving forward. But once I had some momentum built up, it became easier, and the boat stopped swaying around so much. My shoulders and arms were soon aching from pulling the oars through the rough water. They were so blasted heavy.

Eventually, after what felt like hours, the boat passed a tall cliff jutting out into the waves and I saw the light from the lighthouse sweeping across the waves through the mist. Relief flooded over me. I grinned at Kalu over my shoulder. "We're almost at the lighthouse now."

Soon, soon we'd be on solid land. Safe.

Chapter 31

KALU

THE FRONT OF THE boat finally nudged up against a wooden float. Kalu saw that the float was attached to a dock by a sloping ramp.

"All right! We made it. Safe and sound," the tall girl shouted, lowering the oars. "Hey, dude. Can you jump out with the rope and tie us up to that iron ring?"

Kalu scrambled over the boat's front onto the float and tied the rope to an iron ring attached to its edge.

"Here. Tie this one to that other ring." She threw him another rope, one to pull in the boat's stern.

Now the boat was tied snugly against the boards, both front and back.

"I'll just lift your cousin out." She raised Aisha into Kalu's arms. He could feel his cousin trembling with cold and fear.

The girl climbed out of the boat with the big blanket. She tried to help him carry Aisha up the ramp and along the dock. But it was awkward, trying to carry her with someone else. They kept bumping into each other.

"Look, let me do it. I can take her the rest of the way myself," the girl said. "You take the duvet." She carried Aisha up a steep sandy path to a house painted white. He followed with the bulky blanket-like covering.

By the time the girl reached the house she was puffing. She climbed the steps and told him to open the door.

He paused. What if someone was still there?

"It's OK, dude. Really," she told him. "No one's in there. My aunt left with the government men."

So he climbed the steps, cautiously turned the knob and pushed the door open, ready to spring away if anyone tried to nab him.

The girl kicked the door open wider and carried Aisha inside. It was dark and quiet in there. Kalu hesitated in the doorway. The house seemed to be empty.

"Switch on the light," the girl told him.

He stared back at her puzzled. "Light?"

"That switch right there by the door."

He cautiously touched the switch and two overhead lights in the entrance way blazed on as well as some inside the house. He flinched and put his hand up to shield his eyes. Strange. He'd never seen lights like that before. There were lamps on Mister Elliot's boat but they were small and had to be lit one by one.

He stared around the room. Wonders! The room had more shelves filled with way more books than his classroom had. And so many soft-looking places to sit.

"I'll just put your cousin in my bed, then heat some water so we can make a hot drink," the girl said. "But I should probably take off my shoes so I don't make a mess. Maybe you could give your feet a good wipe on the rug here to dry them off."

She kept talking, telling him what she was doing. Somehow her steady voice calmed him.

"My room's back here, just off the kitchen," she went on. "You can follow me if you want. Hold the door open. That's good. There. Aisha will be comfortable here on my bed for a few minutes until we get water warmed up for some hot chocolate."

He followed her to a small room with a bed where she had gently laid Aisha who was fast asleep. She took the blanket from him.

"Too wet. I'll just put this other one on her for now." She covered Aisha with a lighter blanket and spread out the heavy one that Kalu was holding on a chair.

Aisha was snoring but sometimes it sounded as if she was struggling to take in a breath. She'd dropped the pocket watch so it wasn't against her ear now. The girl eased it away and slipped it around her own neck.

"Steam," she whispered to Kalu who was hovering behind

her like an anxious shadow. "I remember someone putting me into a steam bath a long time ago when I was a little kid and had a really bad cold. Wonder who that could have been? Maybe some nanny? We'll get Aisha into a steam bath. That will help her breathing and get her all warmed up. But first, let's have that hot drink."

After a last look at his sleeping cousin, Kalu followed the girl to another room. She spooned brown sweet-smelling powder into two cups and poured hot water from a kettle into them and put the cups on a large table. He sipped the hot beverage. It was so hot it burnt his mouth but it was the most delicious drink he'd ever had. Sweet and chocolaty. There were even biscuits.

"Maureen's oatmeal cookies aren't so bad if you dip them into the hot chocolate like this." The girl demonstrated, showing him how to dip a biscuit into the sweet drink then munch on it.

Yum. The biscuits were so sweet and tasty that Kalu could have eaten a dozen.

But before he'd finished even one of them, the sound of a strangling cough erupted from the bedroom.

The girl dropped her biscuit and they both raced back to the bedroom.

Aisha was choking.

Chapter 32

SPIKE

I LIFTED THE little girl upright so she could catch her breath.

"There, there." I gently rubbed her back. Man, was I turning into an old nurse, or what? Anyway, now she couldn't stop coughing.

"Get some water from the kitchen," I told Kalu.

He dashed back with a cupful of hot water from the kettle.

"It's too hot for her to drink. Get some from the tap. Hurry," I said, frantically.

"Tap?"

"Oh God!" How could anyone not know what a tap was? "You hold her." I thrust the coughing kid into his arms and fled into the kitchen where I grabbed a cup of water from the tap.

"Here. Try this." I held the cup to the little kid's lips. "It'll help your cough."

Eventually she stopped coughing long enough to take a sip. But when she tried to draw in a breath, she started coughing again, her nose streaming.

I wiped her nose with the edge of the pillowcase and gave her some more water. Finally, she stopped coughing and drew in a big ragged breath.

"We better get her into the steam bath right now. It'll help her breathe," I told Kalu. I carried her through to the tiny bathroom. Probably the smallest bathroom I'd ever seen. Whole thing could fit easily into my bedroom closet back home.

I laid the little girl down on the bath mat and ran a bath, not too hot. I didn't want to scald her, but it should be hot enough to create some good steam.

Kalu was standing in the doorway, wide-eyed, as if he'd never seen a bathroom before. Maybe where he came from, they didn't have bathtubs like this.

I was embarrassed to take off the little girl's clothes, especially in front of her boy cousin, so I just lifted her gently into the warm water with her t-shirt and ragged shorts still on. They could use a good washing anyway. She'd lost her shoes, if she'd ever had any.

She took in a deep breath, leaned back and floated in the warm water. She was awake now, her dark brown eyes open, but she was listless. At least she wasn't shivering anymore and had stopped coughing.

When I turned on the tap to add more hot water to the bath, Kalu crept closer and put his hand under the gushing faucet. He smiled in surprise. "Hot!"

"'Course. Don't they have hot-water taps where you're from?"

"Not in my village, no." He shook his head. "I never see this. It is like magic."

I snorted. "Not magic, dude. Every house around here would have hot water coming from a tap. Now how about you make some hot chocolate for your cousin while I take her out of the bath."

After he left, I gently removed the little girl's tattered shirt and shorts and lifted her out of the water, wrapping her skinny body in one of Maureen's big fluffy green towels. The kid's skin was the colour of a Cadbury milk chocolate bar. I patted her short curly hair dry then carried her back to my bedroom and laid her on the bed, still bundled up in the towel. I rummaged through my suitcase for one of my t-shirts. A purple one with an alligator on it. Big enough for a nightshirt on her. I pulled out a plain long-sleeved black one as well.

Kalu came into the bedroom, bearing a cup of hot chocolate.

"Thanks. Why don't you change into this shirt?" I gave him the black one. "It'll be dryer than that hoodie."

He nodded.

"I think you'll like this, Aisha." I propped the little girl up on the pillows and dipped my little finger into the drink to feel it. It didn't feel too hot, so I held it to her lips. She pulled back and blinked up at me, her dark eyes filled with wonder.

"It's good," I told her. "You'll like it. Right, Kalu? She'll like it."

"The drink is plenty good, Aisha. Sweet. So sweet."

So she took a sip but it made her start coughing again.

"She needs medicine," Kalu said.

"I'll see what my aunt has in her medicine cabinet."

I found some cold remedies and Aspirin. Should be good for the kid's fever, I thought. She's so small one adult-sized Aspirin should probably be enough.

The little girl obediently swallowed the pill with some hot chocolate. Then she shut her eyes and snuggled into the quilt I'd borrowed from Maureen's bed.

"We should let her sleep for a while now," I told Kalu. "Sleep is probably the best thing for her." I switched off the lamp and he followed me out of the room. "Let's see what we can find for supper. My aunt said there's some soup in the fridge."

The refrigerator was another surprise for Kalu. He opened the door and blinked at the light then stared wide-eyed at all the boxes and jars inside.

"My guess is you've never seen a refrigerator either," I said.

He shrugged. "Refrigerator." He shook his head. "I do not know that word. We had a cooler box for food on the boat. And another one in the hold for the fish we caught."

I didn't have the energy to explain. I took out a plastic container with "soup" written on the top, dumped the contents into a saucepan and set it on the stove.

Soon we were at the kitchen table with bowls of steaming chicken vegetable soup and slices of Maureen's homemade bread I'd found in the breadbox. "One thing for sure," I muttered. "My aunt's bread's a lot better than her oatmeal cookies. At least I think so."

Kalu didn't answer. He just kept eating steadily until there was no more soup and no more bread left. I guessed that any kind of food would be fine with him.

"Want an apple?" I offered.

"Apple," he repeated. "I have heard of apples. 'A is for Apple,'" he said in a sing-songy voice. "But I never ate one."

"Be my guest." I gave him a red one from the fruit bowl.

He bit into it and chewed, nodding. "Not so good as mango, but good."

"So how about telling me how you and your cousin got to this island. Where did you come from?"

"Um," he hesitated, looking at me warily.

"Look. If you can't trust me, who can you trust?"

As if on cue, there was a burst of coughing from the bedroom. I rushed in. The little girl's face was almost purple as she struggled to catch her breath. I lifted her and stroked her back. "Slowly, kiddo. It's OK." But she couldn't stop coughing. Oh God, is she going to be all right?

I stroked her back some more until she managed to draw in a ragged breath, then another and eventually she stopped coughing, but her breathing was still loud and uneven. Every breath was a struggle. I tried to give her some water but she couldn't drink it. When my hand brushed against her cheek, I found it was burning hot.

"She has a high fever," I told Kalu. He was standing at the doorway, anxiously rubbing his hands together.

He nodded. "Very sick."

I just didn't know what else to do. I'd done everything I knew how. The warm bath, the Aspirin, the drink, keeping her warm under my aunt's heavy quilt. Maybe that was it. Maybe she was too warm now and that was causing her to have a temperature.

"Maybe we should let her cool off. I'll get some cool water and a cloth."

I dipped a face cloth into the bowl of cool water and put it on the girl's forehead as I'd seen them do to sick people in old movies. There was one movie I'd seen on TV not long ago. A Jane Austen story where the younger sister runs out into a storm and comes down with pneumonia or something and almost dies. And her older, more sensible sister spends a lot of time laying cool cloths on her sister's fevered brow. I remembered now: it was called *Sense and Sensibility*.

Trouble was, water was dripping onto the pillow and soon it was soaked. That part wasn't in the movie. I had to send Kalu to the bathroom for another dry towel.

"The Aspirin should help get rid of the fever," I told him.

"Maybe she needs more?" he suggested. "More medicine?"

"You're right. Maybe we can give her one more."

But this time, when the little girl tried to swallow the pill, it set her off coughing again. So I crushed it in a spoon and mixed it into a bit of the chocolate drink. I knelt by the bed on the rug and held the spoon to her mouth. "Come on, Aisha," I coaxed. "Drink this. It'll make you feel better."

After a few minutes, she was able to sip a little of it. Then she shut her eyes and leaned back on the pillow, exhausted, and fell into a deep sleep.

I knelt beside the bed, watching her face. Her eyelashes were curly fringes on her cheeks and her eyebrows were so delicate they looked plucked.

"Guess there's not much else we can do now," I whispered to Kalu. "Just let her sleep." I tucked a light sheet around her and, after turning off the lamp, followed him, tiptoeing out of the room back to the kitchen.

He headed for the outside door.

"You're going somewhere?"

He pulled his flute from his belt. "I play a song for the sun to go down."

As I put the milk back into the fridge, I could hear his music drifting in the open kitchen window. It was a sweet high-pitched melody. A song to the setting sun that had tinged the fog pink.

Chapter 33

KALU

KALU'S STOMACH FELT fuller than it had felt since he left
Mister Elliot's boat. It made him feel warm all over, but on
his way outside he borrowed a jacket. He looked at the boots
beside the door but didn't think his feet would fit.

The setting sun seemed to burrow an orange tunnel
through the fog that had settled around the island. It was low
in the sky, its rim almost touching the sea on the distant
misty horizon.

He stood on one of the big rocks at the edge of the water
and lifted his flute to his lips. He blew into it and found the
goodnight song right away. He played a long version of it
with extra dips and trills until the sun had sunk completely

into the sea, leaving the mist tinged purple.

Then staring out at the waves splashing against the rocks in the twilight, he played a song of gratitude and of hope. He was thankful that he and Aisha were in a warm place now, with what seemed like limitless food and fresh water that gushed from a tap. Both cold and hot. And the tall girl with the strange purple hair seemed to be honest and kind. Thanks for her too. Aisha was resting quietly now and he hoped she would feel better soon.

As the last rays of sunlight reflected pink on the sea, a band of familiar heads popped up near the rocks. The seals again. They had come to check on him, to stare at him as he played the tunes. They seemed to be listening intently to his songs, swaying their heads in the waves.

A deep mournful sound drifted from the tall house with the sweeping light. The sound echoed around the rocks. The girl had told him that it was the foghorn to warn people on the boats about the dangerous reefs around the island, reefs that could be hidden by the fog.

Kalu found that mournful sound on his flute and he used it along with the crashing of the waves on the nearby rocks and the barking of the seals splashing in the water. All sounds for building another song.

A song for remembering his village, his brother, and most of all, for his gentle mother.

It was also a song for this island set in the mist. A song of hope. A song of gratitude. A song for the night.

Chapter 34

SPIKE

I WAS SO WIPED I could hardly stand. I stumbled into the sitting room and collapsed onto the sofa in front of the TV. I switched it on with the remote. News on one station. Nature program about raising chickens on the other. I yawned. Hard to work up enthusiasm about either. I was about to nod off when Kalu came back inside.

"Don't know about you, dude, but I'm so beat I could sleep for a week." I stretched my feet onto the wooden coffee table strewn with books and magazines.

He sat beside me on the sofa, eyes wide with amazement. I guess TV was another thing he'd never experienced, but I was too tired to ask him about it. Or about why he liked to play his flute to the setting sun. In fact, I was too tired to ask him about anything.

I curled up at one end of the sofa and propped a cushion under my head. No idea what was on TV now. Chicken program replaced by a documentary about building boats, maybe? Couldn't keep my eyes open. I sighed and fell asleep.

A loud boom shook the house. My eyes snapped open. Too dark to see anything. Lights were off. So was the TV.

I rushed to the window. Waves were crashing on the rocks, hurling curtains of spray skyward into the fog. Something seriously different out there. What? It hit me. The lighthouse. It was a tall dark shadow against the foggy sky. No light was sweeping around it. The lamp was out.

No! This couldn't be happening. The lamp couldn't be out. Not on such a stormy night. That's when boaters needed it most.

"Kalu!" I shook him. How could anyone sleep through all that noise? "Kalu! Wake up! The lighthouse lamp. It's out. We have to fix it."

"What? What?"

"I need your help, dude. Now."

He rubbed his eyes and slid off the end of the sofa. He followed me to the door where I stamped on a pair of Maureen's rubber boots. I grabbed her raincoat and a flashlight by the key rack. I threw another raincoat at him.

I pulled the door open. The fierce wind jerked it out of my grasp and it crashed against the wall. Kalu stumbled out hanging onto the flapping coat. It took all my strength to force the door closed after us. I switched on the flashlight only to see swirls of dense fog and rain, but we dashed through it toward the lighthouse. I tripped in the too-big boots and fell heavily onto my knees, the flashlight bashing my chin. Kalu bumped into me and we were both down.

"Oof," he muttered. "Sorry."

"OK, we got to be careful here." I scrambled up and kept going, bent into the wind and rain.

The fog was so thick and the night so dark that with the weak light from the flashlight neither of us could see much of anything. We had to feel our way in the dark. Finally, we reached the lighthouse. I felt along its stone wall for the door. There it was. Flapping open. Latch must be off. Surprising, after that speech Maureen had made about always making sure the outside door was shut and latched firmly against the weather. I held it for Kalu and followed him inside, forcing the door shut behind us.

"Up the stairs," I panted. "We have to climb the stairs. To check what's wrong with the lamp." I scrambled up the winding stairs with him right behind. At the top, I flicked the flashlight's dim beam around. The big lamp wasn't rotating. Wasn't even turned on. Everything was totally dark. Quiet too. No foghorn.

"Cupboard's around here. Somewhere." I tried to catch my breath as I felt around the wall. "Where Maureen keeps her tools."

"Ah-ha!" My fingers found the cupboard. Working the latch loose, I eased the door open. "Flashlight. One with a good beam. Must be one in here. Yes!" I flicked on a heavy yellow flashlight. It lit up the lighthouse room.

"You fix the light?" Kalu blinked against the sudden brightness.

"Don't really know what to do." I flashed the beam around the big lamp. "Where to start . . ."

Then it hit me. "The generator!" The constant hum of the generator motor wasn't there. "I can't hear it. It's down the stairs. Let's check it out."

We clambered back down. At the bottom of the stairs, I felt around for the generator enclosure. It felt wet. Must have got wet when the outside door had flapped open.

I flashed the beam into the enclosure. Silence! The generator was dead, all right. An unpleasant smell stung my nose. What was it? Was the smell connected somehow?

"Maybe it's out of fuel." But when I checked the fuel tank, the indicator was at the halfway mark. "No. Still plenty of diesel. And the hose coming out of the tank hasn't come loose." I showed Kalu where the hose left the tank.

"But look," he said, his eyes huge.

Diesel was leaking from where the fuel hose went into the generator.

"So that must be the problem. Not enough fuel was getting into the generator. Hold the flashlight, will you? Shine it down here on the hose." I tried to stuff the hose back onto the motor but it wouldn't stay.

"Duct tape," I told him. "We need a wad of good sticky duct tape. Hold the hose onto the motor while I get some, OK?"

"OK."

I snatched the flashlight from him and scrambled back up the stairs to search for a roll of silvery tape. Found some in the tool cupboard. I grabbed it and clattered back down the stairs where I tore off a strip.

"Can you wind the tape around the hose and attach it to the generator? I'll hold the flashlight for you." By now the flashlight's beam had become weaker. I tried to thump some life into it. "Wind it good and tight now."

Kalu nodded and after three or four more strips, he had the hose attached.

"Good." I thumped the flashlight again to try to get more light.

"Now?" he asked.

"Now we have to start up the motor. Says start on this button here." I pressed the button. The motor turned over. "Yes!" I said.

But it coughed a few times and died. I pressed the starter again. Same thing.

"Why won't the stupid thing start? I'm sure it's getting fuel now." I checked the motor with the flashlight's dying beam. There, surrounded by strips of duct tape from previous repairs, was a tap painted red.

"Oh, right. Now I remember Maureen saying something about having to turn on this tap before pushing the starter. Something about purging the hose." I turned it on all the way, and this time Kalu pressed the starter button. Still didn't start. He pushed it again and again. Finally, the motor in the generator coughed into life and started. But now it was running so fast and loud it sounded like it would shake itself right out of its housing. I tried easing back on the red tap. Soon the motor was humming along with its usual calm hum.

"We did it!" I grinned at Kalu. "We friggin' did it, dude!" I could barely see him grinning back in the feeble light from the flashlight. "Let's check the lamp upstairs."

As we dashed back up the stairs, feeling our way now because the flashlight was dead, the big lighthouse lamp sprang into life. Yellow light bounced off the walls.

I took in a deep breath of relief. Now I could see Kalu's wide grin plain as day. The foghorn sounded out its mournful call. It was working too.

"Let's just check that the generator's still OK." We retraced our steps. So much easier now we could see where we were going. "Maybe we should stick on more tape to be sure that fuel hose doesn't come loose again."

"OK." He picked up the duct tape.

One thing bothering me was Maureen had said she'd put the lamp on "automatic." So when the generator failed, why hadn't the emergency batteries kicked in? While Kalu was plastering the generator with more tape, I checked around the outside door and found out why.

"Look at this. The wires to the box of emergency batteries are completely soaked. They must have got wet and shorted out when the door blew open in the storm. Well, that explains why the emergency batteries didn't kick in."

"Is enough tape?" he asked.

The hose bulging with tape looked like a python that had just swallowed a giant rat.

"Perfect. Let's go back to the house." I made sure that I latched the door firmly before leaving.

With the fog pulsing with light around us from the revolving lighthouse lamp, we ploughed our way through the stiff wind and rain, back to the house.

Kalu followed me like a zombie and collapsed onto the sofa as if he'd never left it. He curled up and closed his eyes.

The TV was blaring some rowdy game show. I clicked it off and went to check on Aisha. She was still breathing, so I stumbled back through the living room to Maureen's bedroom where I fell in a heap onto her bed. In spite of the raging sea and the waves crashing on the rocks, I was asleep before I could even turn over.

The next sound I heard was the drone of a boat motor.

Maureen was back. Already!

Sunlight poured through Maureen's bedroom window. Morning!

I jumped off her bed, quickly smoothed her covers and rushed to the living room to peer out the window facing the dock.

Sure enough, a boat was approaching the dock. Seamus's water taxi. So early.

Kalu was still curled up asleep on the sofa, his head in his same green woolly hat half-hidden by a cushion.

"Kalu!" I shook him. "My aunt's here. With Seamus."

He leapt off the sofa and flew to the window. We could see Seamus in the bow of his boat steering, his old seaman hat pulled low on his brow.

Kalu shook his head. He looked scared. "Aisha," he said.

I followed him to the bedroom.

Where was Aisha? The bed was a tangle of blankets and pillows. The little kid had burrowed under and just the back of her curly hair was visible. Was she OK?

I felt her neck. Warm, but not as fiery hot as last night. How could she breathe, buried in blankets like that?

I lifted them away and stared down at the side of the little girl's sleeping face. She had pulled through the night, so did that mean she was going to recover? In the Jane Austen story, it did. They talked about the fever breaking or something.

But Maureen was already here. She'd said she'd be back early, but the crack of dawn was crazy.

How could I tell her about the kids?

May as well go and get it over with.

Chapter 35

KALU

AS SOON AS THE girl left, Kalu hurried back to the bedroom.

"Aisha. Aisha. You have to wake up now." He patted her back, trying not to panic. "The girl's aunt is back. And a man is with her. A man wearing a police hat."

Aisha lifted her head from the pillow and shook it, squeezing her eyes. "Still so sleepy, sleepy," she murmured.

She looked tired but she didn't look as sick as she did yesterday. And she wasn't coughing now.

"We have to go quick," he told her. "Come now, before the girl's aunt and the policeman come here to the house and find us."

Aisha reluctantly slipped off the bed, yawning and blinking. She pulled the big green bath towel around her back like a shawl and padded after him to the living room.

He peered out the window again. The storm had passed. The fog had lifted, leaving a blue sky, and it looked as if the wind had dropped.

"Everyone is still down at the boat," he told Aisha. "Even the girl. We'll have time to get away if we hurry. Let's go."

"But why do we have to leave?"

"That policeman. We don't know him. He's probably come to catch us. To take us away. Maybe put us in prison like Mister Elliot said."

Kalu slipped out the door, down the steps, and along the path to the tall house. He kept his head down and hustled Aisha away.

He hoped that no one from the boat would spot them.

"Kalu." Soon Aisha was trailing behind. "Where are we going, Kalu?"

"We'll go back to our beach on the other side of the island," he whispered. "I know the way."

They would go up along the path through the bushes past the tall house. Then right across the top of the island to the other side, back to their cave hideout. And the beach where the fisherman had dropped them off.

"Maybe Mister Elliot is there right now with his boat, come to pick us up." He urged Aisha along. "Maybe he's searching for us, wondering where we are."

They had to hurry to catch him before he left.

Chapter 36

SPIKE

"HEY, MAUREEN!" I waved at her down at the dock. Tried to look casual, as if I wasn't harbouring a couple of runaways. Or whatever they were.

"Spike! I'm surprised you're up so early. Everything OK last night?"

"Sure, everything's fine, considering . . ."

"Considering what?"

"Well, um. The generator conked out because the fuel line came loose. So the lighthouse lamp went out. But we, I mean, I fixed it."

"Oh no! Didn't the emergency batteries take over?"

I shook my head. "Battery wires got soaked when the door blew open in the storm so they must have shorted out. Anyways, everything's good now."

"But I thought I left the door well latched. Oh, Spike. Good thing you were here on the island, after all. Goodness! You're a real hero. A lifesaver, so you are. I mean it literally. No telling how many boats were out there in the storm and would have crashed if the light was down all night. How did you even know how fix the fuel line?"

I shrugged. It was great feeling I'd done something right for once. But all her enthusiasm was a bit embarrassing.

Just wait until she found out about the kids . . .

Seamus was looking at me with raised eyebrows. Did he just wink? It's like he knew something fishy was going on. Was he warning me not to tell Maureen about the kids? Why would he do that? How would he even know about them?

"The new generator's really heavy," Maureen said. "Can you give us a hand? Think you're up to it so early in the morning?"

"I guess."

The generator was still in its cardboard box. It could have been a piano, it was so heavy and awkward to lift out of the boat. Finally, we levered it over the gunnels and it crashed onto the landing float causing it to lurch.

"Can you bring us the moving cart, Spike? It's in the shed."

Shifting the box onto the big moving cart was another challenge. When we got it on, I held it and pushed while

Seamus pulled it up the ramp backwards and along the dock. Maureen followed with her arms full of grocery bags and headed for the house.

"Um, Maureen. There's something . . ." I started to tell her about the kids, but Seamus coughed. Was he shaking his head, warning me?

Oh well, she'll find out about them soon enough. Nothing I could do about it now. I braced myself, waiting for the questions to start.

But miracle of friggin' miracles! She just dropped the grocery bags on the stairs leading to the door and followed us along the path to the lighthouse.

"I'll show you where to put the new generator." She directed us into the workshop. "I see you used a fair bit of our trusty duct tape on the fuel line, Spike. Good thinking."

I nodded and glanced over my shoulder. No sign of the kids. Yet.

"Let's set it down right over here and we'll see about switching over the wires. The sooner we get the new one connected, the better I'll feel. We can't operate the lighthouse without a reliable generator, right?"

"Right," I grunted as Seamus and I shoved the bulky generator off the moving cart while she held the cart steady.

I was getting more and more panicky about how to tell her about the kids. One thing for sure, I didn't want to do it in front of Seamus. Although I had a feeling he already knew. It was like his dark eyes could penetrate my brain and know all my secrets.

"Let me help you move the old one out," he offered Maureen. "Then I can connect the new one for you."

"Thanks very much, Seamus. Then we won't have to wait until Sloan and Thomas return." Maureen cut the box open with box cutters and the three of us pulled away the cardboard and dragged the new generator close enough to the old one so we could switch the wires.

"How about a cup of tea, Seamus?" Maureen said. "I really could use one. Feels as though we left the village in the middle of the night to get back here."

"If Lela's girl could help me with the connections, I would not say no to that." He smiled at me.

So I stayed in the lighthouse with Seamus, handing him screwdrivers and wrenches, as he disconnected the wires and hoses from the old generator and connected them to the shiny new one.

"And this wire will go right in here to the negative pole," he said. "The main thing is to be sure all the wires are going to the right place."

I tried to concentrate on what he was doing, but I was still bracing for an angry Maureen, rushing back to ask me about the kids, demanding an immediate explanation. But she didn't come. Weird. Very weird.

Seamus heaved the old generator aside and I helped him push the new one into its place. After connecting fresh wires from the emergency box to the new generator, it was finally installed.

"Want to start it?" he asked me.

I pressed the starter button and it instantly started humming away. Sounded perfect. "What should we do with the old generator? Dump it?"

"I think Maureen will want to keep it for parts. You never know. As I said, the Isle of Last Chance is a beginning place, all whirling and spinning —"

"Tea's ready," Maureen called.

The old man led the way back to the house.

I dreaded going in. Dreaded the big uncomfortable scene Maureen was going to make about the kids. I followed Seamus inside, braced for an explosion.

But nothing happened.

Kalu was gone.

I checked the bedroom.

Aisha was gone too.

Both kids had disappeared.

Without a trace.

Without a friggin' trace.

Chapter 37

KALU

"COME ON, AISHA. We have to hurry. We have to get away before they see us. Before they catch us. That policeman."

Kalu helped Aisha climb up the rocky trail through the thick bushes behind the lighthouse. It was steep and she stumbled so he had to almost carry her partway. He knew the trail would take them up over the top of the island and back down to the other side, to the little bay where Mister Elliot had dropped them off. Back to the cave where they could hide.

A cold wind blew from the water, carrying a salty spray. Aisha shivered and pulled the towel around her shoulders more tightly. She started coughing and had to stop to catch her breath, wheezing.

Maybe he should have left her behind in the girl's warm bed. But no. The girl's aunt and that policeman would have found her. Then they would have thrown her into prison. That's what Mister Elliot said they'd do.

Mister Elliot. He might be waiting to collect them from the beach right now. Right this very minute. Wondering where they were. He should never have agreed to go with the girl yesterday.

"Hurry, Aisha," he urged her. "Mister Elliot might be waiting for us."

Aisha was on her hands and knees, struggling to climb an especially steep section of the trail. He held her hand and pulled her up and around a rock.

When they finally reached the top of the cliff and the trail levelled out, she was panting hard.

"Can we stop? For a rest? My chest. Hurts so much. When I breathe." Her face was shiny with sweat. She couldn't go any further.

Kalu looked around. Way off the trail was a pile of rocks beside a stunted tree. "We could go and shelter behind those rocks for a minute until you feel better." He led her off the trail and through the long grass and shrubs. If they hunkered down behind the rocks, they would be sheltered from the biting wind. And they'd be hidden from the girl's aunt and the policeman.

His stomach growled. He should have grabbed some food from the kitchen. But when he saw that the girl's aunt had already come back, and she had brought a policeman with her, he panicked. His only thought was to sneak out of the house and escape. Escape to the other side of the island.

And hope with all his might that Mister Elliot was there with his boat, waiting to rescue them.

Chapter 38

SPIKE

I CHECKED UNDER my bed. Just wet jeans and dust balls. Checked the closet, the bathroom.

"Looking for something, love?" Maureen asked as she carried a tray with a pot of fresh tea and a package of buns to the table.

"Something? Um, my other shoes. Have you seen them?"

"Is that them in the sitting room under the TV?"

"Oh, right. Thanks." I picked them up, checking behind the sofa. Just more dust balls.

"What a mess in the kitchen," Maureen said. "But I'm glad you found the soup in the fridge. You must have liked it, having two bowls of it?"

Two dirty bowls from Kalu's and my supper were still on the table with a bunch of crumbs from the bread. "Sorry." I put the bowls into the sink. "Guess I was too tired last night to wash up."

"Two hot chocolate cups too. If we weren't way off on an island, miles from anywhere, I'd think you had company last night, so I would," Maureen chuckled. "Did the Selkies join you for a late-night party?"

I forced my lips to smile weakly at her joke. Then I frowned. I couldn't understand it. Where were the kids? How could they have disappeared just like that? If it weren't for the dirty dishes and messy bedroom, I could almost believe I'd just dreamt up the whole thing.

Now what should I do? If the kids managed to escape, they obviously didn't want to be discovered. So how could I tell Maureen about them? Especially in front of Seamus.

I poured myself a steaming cup of tea, and after adding milk and sugar, sat opposite Seamus at the kitchen table. As I stirred my tea, I kept thinking about the kids. I didn't want to be a fink. On the other hand, I told myself, Aisha's really sick. She might even have pneumonia, or something worse. And camping out in some cold dark cave again was the very last thing such a sick kid should be doing. Maybe I should tell Maureen.

Besides, how were they going to get back to their cave without a boat?

Then I remembered seeing Kalu a few evenings ago near the lighthouse playing his flute to the setting sun. So there must be a trail that goes overland from the lighthouse to their cave.

After breakfast I'll go out there and find that trail, I told myself. Then I'll find the kids and convince Kalu he had no choice. He had to let Maureen know that he and his cousin were here. What's the big secret anyway? He still hadn't told me where they'd come from. Or who they were hiding from. And what they were doing on this desolate island, so far from anywhere.

Seamus's phone rang. He checked it and said, "I must go now. Thank you for the tea and buns, Maureen."

"Thank you for your help. I feel much safer now with the new generator."

"Goodbye, Lela's girl." Seamus nodded his grey head to me and put on his tattered seaman's hat as he left the kitchen. "You will make the best choice. Always the best choice."

It's like he knew exactly what I was thinking.

I sipped my tea and felt my mother's watch in its pouch.

"Oh! I remember that pouch," Maureen said, coming back to the table with the refilled teapot. "Your mother made it in our last year at school in a craft class."

"She made this pouch herself?" Now it was really special.

Maureen nodded and refilled my cup. She reached for the pouch examining the design on it. "The triskelion. It's an ancient symbol, thousands of years old. People have found it carved in caves all over Ireland. It's a powerful symbol, we were always told. Sort of emblem to protect people on journeys."

I thought of Kieran and the travellers I'd met in Dublin. "I still have her watch." I slid the watch out of the pouch, its silver casing catching the light. "Still works if I don't forget to wind it."

"Oh!" Maureen's eyes were shiny and she shook her head sadly. "I remember when your mother received that watch. Her father gave it to her for her sixteenth birthday. I think she always treasured it especially, because that was just before he died."

"How did he die?"

"Has your father never told you about him?"

"My father didn't ever tell me anything." I shrugged. "Actually he's never even told me much about my mother. He was always busy with his business, and we didn't have exactly the best relationship especially after Felicity came along."

"Oh, you poor love." Her lips curved down and she patted my arm. "About your grandfather, it was really sad, so it was. He was on his way home from work one night and was caught in the crossfire of a skirmish with the IRA. Killed outright. After that happened your mother couldn't wait to leave Ireland. She got a job as a nanny for a family in Toronto and met your father there a couple of years later. He was crazy about her. Love at first sight, he always said. They were married before she was twenty. He got some special immigration papers for her so she could."

"I didn't know about all that."

Maureen yawned. "Oh dear. It was pitch dark when I got

up this morning. I was worried about leaving you on the island on your own. Here I am, ready for my afternoon nap and it's not yet ten o'clock. I'll check the lamp in the lighthouse and the messages, then I'll have a bit of a toes-up time, if you don't mind washing up?"

Chapter 39

KALU

AISHA CURLED UP under the green towel between the rocks and shut her eyes.

"Don't fall asleep, Aisha." Kalu nudged her arm. "As soon as you've rested up, we'll have to go back to the trail to reach our cave. Remember?"

Aisha seemed to be trying to force her eyes open. She nodded then slumped down behind a rock even more.

Kalu sighed. He didn't know what to do. Maybe he should try carrying her? But could he carry her all the way across to the other side of the island?

A shadow flitted over them. He looked up. A bird with

huge outstretched wings was circling above them. In the fields around his village he'd seen huge birds sweep down on a dead creature. Or one about to die. Was it one of those birds?

Maybe it was his small cousin it was smelling . . .

"Go away!" he shouted at the bird, his heart beating fast. "Leave us alone."

But the bird croaked down at him and circled closer and closer. It landed on the top of the stunted tree close by. Flapping its giant wings and tilting its head, it stared down at him.

In the sky, another bird appeared. It circled, coming closer as well.

"Come on, Aisha," Kalu urged his cousin. "We have to move from here."

She nodded then sighed and made no attempt to get up.

He tried to lift her but she rolled away.

"Just a short little sleep, please, please," she mumbled.

The bird squawked and ruffled its feathers, its beady eyes still on them.

Kalu threw a pebble at it to try to drive it away. The pebble missed and the bird squawked some more, even louder. But it didn't leave.

Now the second bird landed on a bush. And that bush was even closer. It was at least as huge and scary as the first bird. It flexed its spiky claws and stared down at Kalu as well.

Kalu searched around for a stick. All he could find was a

twig with withered leaves still clinging to it. "Go away," he shouted at the birds, shaking the twig at them. "Get away from here."

But they clicked their beaks, sharp and pointy as knives, and muttered at him, flapping wings as enormous as blankets.

He stood in front of his cousin, shielding her from the birds' view. His heart was thumping hard now. He waved his twig at them again. "Go away!" he shouted at them. "There's nothing for you here. Go!"

Both birds stared down at him and squawked back, snapping their beaks.

They shuffled along the branches even closer.

Chapter 40

SPIKE

I WASHED THE BREAKFAST dishes as fast as I could. Then I grabbed the rest of the breakfast buns in their plastic bag, threw on a fleece vest and headed for the trail behind the lighthouse. I stopped at the lighthouse.

"Maureen!" I called up the spiral staircase. My voice echoed off the stone sides.

"Yes?" Maureen's voice came back.

"I'm going for a walk up the cliff trail behind the lighthouse."

"All right. But watch your step. It's pretty steep in parts, so it is."

"See you later."

The trail started just past the two white crosses for Maureen's Gerry and Peter. It zigzagged back and forth at a slope so steep in some places that I had to grab onto some weeds to haul myself up. It headed upwards between purple heather and other scrubby bushes until it reached the top of a cliff.

When I turned around and looked out to the water, past the island's cliffs, there was no land in sight. Just the earth's distant curve way out to sea, melting until it was lost in the grey clouds. Next fall of land would be what? Friggin' Newfoundland? What a thought!

I'd better hurry. The sooner I found the kids, the better. As I turned back to the trail, wind swirled around me so I zipped the fleece vest up to my neck. The trail led away from the coast, toward the middle of the island. I was right, I thought. It must go to the other side where the kids had been hiding out in the cave. Maybe that's where they were heading now. Or maybe they'd found some other hideout.

I scanned the dense bushes on both sides of the path. No sign of them.

Bushes soon made way for a few spindly trees here and there. I pulled in a deep breath. Smelled good up here. Fresh and sweet. The wind brought salt air that mixed with the scent of purple heather just starting to bloom.

"Kalu, Aisha," I shouted into the wind. "I've got food for you. Delicious buns . . ." I held up the bag of buns in case they were spying from behind a bush or rock.

I moved slowly along the trail, listening hard, eyes peeled. Nothing.

The trail led up to the very top of the island. I hunkered down on a rock and stared at the view. From this high point, I could see in all directions. Behind me, looking what must be west, because that's where the sun set, was nothing but ocean. Straight ahead, east of the island, I could catch a glimpse of the hilly mainland on the other side of the broad strait.

"Kalu, Aisha! Food. I've got something delicious for you," I called out again.

Still no one. No movement except for bushes rustling in the wind.

No. What was that? A bird. A big black bird was circling overhead with wings outstretched, eyes searching the low bushes. It wasn't a gull. Maybe some kind of hawk or eagle?

It looked as if it had caught sight or smell of something hiding in the bushes. Creepy. I remembered seeing a TV documentary about some sort of raptor and how they could smell food or carrion from miles away.

As I watched, another big bird swooped down to join the first, huge outstretched wings wobbling in the air currents, head craning forward, eyes searching, searching. And there was another bird. And another. A whole gang of friggin' predators.

Close up, the birds were gigantic and terrifying with enormous wings. They looked big enough to snatch an animal.

Or a small child.

"Aisha! Kalu!" I shouted. More urgently now. Had the birds spotted the kids?

One of the birds landed on a tall tree near a pile of rocks. It ruffled its feathers and croaked. Drew up its shoulders in a menacing way and stared this way and that.

I picked up a long stick and headed for the bird, swinging the stick to warn it to stay away. Its huge talons looked sharp enough to scratch out my eyes. It seemed as though it was getting ready to pounce but I kept wading through the bushes, straight at it. The bushes were so thick and prickly I had to bash my way through them.

Before I got to that vicious-looking bird, the other two birds swooped over my head. They turned and glided back toward me in lazy circles, closer and closer.

I hunched my shoulders, expecting one of them to grab the top of my hair with its talons. One landed on a tall rock about three metres away. It folded its wings and stared down at me with unblinking eyes. Talk about eerie! This was starting to feel like a Hitchcock movie.

"Go away," I hissed, waving my stick at it. "Scat, you friggin' bird. Get lost."

It stretched its talons and squawked back at me. But it didn't move away.

Then behind a pile of rocks, I saw a flash. A green woolly hat!

"Kalu! I've got to talk to you." I stepped toward the rocks.

"I'm alone. See. No one's with me. And I've brought food. Some buns. Delicious sweet buns."

At the mention of food, his whole head appeared. His dark eyes watched me as I moved nearer. Looked as if he was ready to take off any second.

"Some bread for you and Aisha." I held out the bag and smiled a big friendly smile. "Sweet bread. Bet you're starving."

"You are alone?"

"'Course, dude. That's what I said." I climbed down over the rocks. "But where's Aisha?"

He nodded toward a bush behind him. Sure enough, crouched under it was the little girl, one of Maureen's green towels bundled around her.

I rushed past the birds to her side. She was breathing heavily and a film of sweat covered her forehead. "Are you hungry, kiddo?" I wiped her face with a corner of the towel.

She didn't say anything but Kalu squatted beside me and stared at the bag of buns.

"Here. Have one." I handed him a large sticky bun. Its sweet top was shiny and it was filled with juicy raisins.

In a second, the bun was gone. Like he'd swallowed it whole. I gave him another, then broke one in half to try to feed the little girl. Although she was sick, she managed to nibble and swallow a few bites. Between the two kids, soon not a scrap of food was left. None for the gang of big scary birds who were still hovering close by.

Kalu sighed when he saw the bag was empty.

"Lots more food down at the lighthouse, you know," I told him. "My aunt's cupboards are full."

"We cannot go there."

"You really have to, dude. For one thing, it's not fair to Aisha. She's sick and will just get sicker out here in this cold wind unless she gets good care and can rest where she'll be warm."

Kalu shook his head.

"Why don't you want to come with me?"

"Your aunt. She brought the policeman."

"Police? You mean Seamus? No, he's not a policeman. He's a water taxi driver. Anyway, he's gone now."

"Maybe your aunt. When she sees us. She will call the police."

"No, I don't think she would. I'd tell her not to. Anyway, you could explain to her why you're here on the island and where you've come from, and all that. She's actually pretty nice, and she'd probably understand. She could help you, you know."

I talked and talked but Kalu still shook his head.

"Danger. Too much danger. And also, the man with the boat, Mister Elliot, will come back for us. Maybe today he will come. Maybe he is there now."

I knew the man wouldn't come back. If he was going to, he'd have returned a long time ago. But there was no convincing Kalu about that.

I sighed. I was getting tired of this. Why should I care so much anyway?

Aisha coughed. She was so little. So thin. I *had* to do something to get her help.

So I tried something else. "My aunt's a great cook, you know, dude. I bet she'll be making something delicious for supper tonight. Maybe even a pie. Do you like apple pie and ice cream? So absolutely delicious."

Aisha coughed some more. She coughed and coughed and her breath came in ragged wheezes that sounded like they were rattling her chest.

I knelt beside her and stroked her back. Why hadn't I brought some water?

Finally, the little girl stopped coughing and used the edge of the towel to wipe her runny nose before curling up under it, exhausted.

"Look, dude." I stared up into Kalu's concerned eyes. "Don't you see how sick your little cousin is? She needs help. Right now."

Still he hesitated.

"Look. If you bring Aisha to my aunt's house, nothing bad will happen to either of you. I promise. With all my heart, I promise you." I patted my chest and tried to look as convincing as I could. There must be something I could do to persuade him. My hand touched my mother's pouch. I pulled it from around my neck. "See my mother's watch?"

He nodded.

"Here's the deal. If you come back to my aunt's place, I'll give the watch to you." I offered it to him.

His eyebrows arched up to his woolly hat as he stared at me.

"Take it, dude," I urged him. "You can have it."

He took the pouch and pulled it over his head. He patted it and for a long moment, he didn't say anything.

"Please, please come with me." I was hoping with all my might.

"Come, Aisha." He made up his mind. "We go with the girl." Helping her up, he bundled the towel around her shoulders like a cape.

She could barely walk, she was so weak and trembling.

"You'll like my aunt. I know you will." I grinned with relief at them both.

Kalu led the way through the thick shrubs toward the trail.

When the scary birds saw we were moving, they shook their feathers and grumbled and squawked.

"Go on," I yelled at them.

"Go away," Kalu yelled, too, shaking a twig at them.

They spread their wings and all flew up into the air together with a whoosh that sounded like air escaping from a giant gas tank.

The little girl was watching them fly off in ever-increasing circles above us. She tripped on a root and fell to her knees. Holding her cheek, she whimpered. A sharp branch had scratched her face.

"It's just a scratch, Aisha." I knelt beside her and patted the little girl's cheek with the towel. "How about if I carry you to the trail?" I lifted her but it was hard going between the bushes. I needed both hands to push the branches away so I put the girl down again. "How about I'll piggyback you?"

"Piggyback?"

"Here. Climb up on my back." I squatted in front of her. The little girl clambered up and hung onto my shoulders. "There. That's better." Soon we were back on the dirt trail.

The kid was so small and light that I kept carrying her all the way back down the steep trail to the lighthouse. Kalu straggled behind.

"Maureen," I called when I reached the lighthouse. I un-latched the door and shouted up the stairs. "Maureen, are you there? Here's someone I'd like you to meet."

Chapter 41

KALU

HE SHOULD NEVER have agreed to return to the house with the girl. What if it was a trap? What if the aunt had called the police? What if they were right there in the house, waiting to grab him and Aisha?

But he followed the girl down the trail, ready to take off any second. She had Aisha on her back.

He clasped the girl's leather watch case swinging from his neck. He knew the watch was important to her. It had been her mother's. So giving it to him must mean that she would keep her promise and not let anything bad happen to him and Aisha.

Still, his heart was hammering in his chest.

The girl had opened the door of the tall house for the light and was calling up into it, but no one was answering. Maybe her auntie had gone away again. He hoped so. Maybe they would be alone, and the girl would give them some food, some sweet chocolate tea. He was hungry.

But he was always hungry. It was as if a lively puppy lived inside his belly, always whimpering for food.

Hush, he told his belly, patting it. He looked past the girl into the light's house. Beside the stairs where they'd repaired the old generator the night before, sat a new one in its enclosure, painted a shiny yellow and connected with new wires.

"Maybe your auntie has gone away now?" he said.

"No, I don't think so. She's probably gone back to the house. She said she wanted to take a nap." The girl shut the door and latched it, then headed to the house still carrying Aisha on her back.

Kalu sighed. He had no choice. He had to follow them.

But he was ready to take off any second.

Chapter 42

SPIKE

"MAUREEN," I CALLED, coming in the door. I glanced back. Kalu was still trailing way behind. "Come on, dude. You have to meet her."

"I'm in the kitchen," Maureen called back.

I got my face ready for her surprise.

"What?" Maureen dropped the knife she was using to chop vegetables and rushed forward. "Who? Who have you got here?"

"This is Aisha." I slid the kid off my back onto a chair beside the table. I returned to the front door and hauled Kalu inside. "And this is her cousin, Kalu."

Maureen followed me through the living room. "But, but . . ." She looked behind Kalu out the door. "I didn't hear a boat. Your parents?"

"The kids are here on the island alone, as far as I know."

"Oh, mercy!" Maureen's hands flew to her face. "Well, do come in. What did you say the boy's name is?"

"Kalu. And his cousin's Aisha. I found them on the other side of the island a couple days ago."

"What? A couple of days ago? And you didn't tell me?"

I shrugged and flicked the hair out of my eyes.

"You said they were alone?"

I nodded.

"But how did they get to the island? Where have they come from? What are they doing here?"

"I don't know. Kalu said a fisherman dropped them off because it was getting too dangerous for them to be on his boat."

"Maybe they're connected to those migrants on the news who've been trying to escape from Africa," Maureen said.

"Could be. When I found them, they were hiding in a cave and Aisha was sick with a bad cold but now she's even sicker. So I convinced them to come back here with me last night. I, um, picked them up in your boat."

Maureen's eyes were huge with wonder. "Ah, that explains the extra bowls and cups this morning, so it does." She shook her head. "But come through to the kitchen now, Kalu, and we'll sort this out, somehow."

Aisha's hacking cough interrupted Maureen. I followed her through the living room and back into the kitchen, urging Kalu along.

Aisha coughed and coughed, wheezing between, trying to catch her breath.

Maureen hurried to the sink for a cup of water that she held out to Aisha, stroking her back. Finally she stopped coughing and, as she took a sip, Maureen's face was filled with such deep concern I knew at that instant I didn't have to worry about my aunt turning the kids out into the cold. A huge weight lifted from my shoulders. I knew, no matter what happened, she'd look after them.

Aisha pulled the towel closer around herself and shivered. I wasn't sure if it was from being cold or scared.

"This little one's needing some warm clothes." Maureen's voice was soft with worry. "Maybe a warm bath too."

"I gave her a bath last night, then she slept in my bed. But when you and Seamus came back this morning, they took off again. Now Kalu's really scared you'll call the police."

Kalu was staring at my aunt warily. He looked as though at any second he was about to bolt away through the door.

"But I told him you wouldn't. I promised him you wouldn't call the police or anyone. So you won't, right?"

Maureen stared back at the boy. "All right, I won't call anyone. Not at the moment anyway. But you must tell us your whole story, Kalu. Where you came from, and exactly how you got to the island. But first, let's get the little girl warmed up in the bath. Look how she's trembling, poor little mite."

It was true that Aisha was shivering even more now.

"Then we'll get her into some warm dry clothes," Maureen went on. "Is that your t-shirt she's wearing?"

"I gave it to her last night."

Maureen lifted the kid to carry her into the bathroom and Aisha's eyes widened with fright.

"It's all right, Aisha." I tried to reassure her. "A bath will warm you up. You liked it last night, remember? Kalu and me, we'll be right out here waiting for you."

I managed to lure Kalu into the kitchen to the table with a banana and a glass of orange juice.

Soon the little girl came out of the bathroom, bathed and wrapped in a dry towel, with Maureen holding her hand.

"All right if I put her into your bed, Spike?"

"Of course." I rummaged through my suitcase for another dry t-shirt and pulled out a dark blue one for her.

Once she was tucked into bed and given some lemon tea sweetened with plenty of honey and another Aspirin, Maureen said, "We'll leave the door open for you, love, so if you need anything else, just call us."

"Now, you two." She came to the table, her arms crossed and a stern look on her face. "Let's have the whole story."

I grinned at her. "I can tell you my part, but there's a whole lot I don't know. Good luck prying it out of Mr. Closed-mouth, here."

After I explained how I'd first met the kids and convinced

them to come to the lighthouse with me, then how they'd run away this morning, and how I'd tracked them down again on the cliffs, I turned to Kalu. "Now it's over to you, dude. Tell us where you two came from. And how you got here."

Kalu sucked in his lips and stared at the floor. Finally, he cleared his throat and said, "It was a fisherman. He bring us here."

"A fisherman?" Maureen said.

"Yes. And he say, he tell us, stay here on this island and he will come back for us in a couple days, he say."

"But he didn't return?"

Kalu shook his head. "We have some water and some matches, a little food. But that is many days ago. We wait and wait, Aisha and me."

Maureen nodded, encouraging him to go on.

"Then Aisha, she get sick, so sick she wants to sleep and sleep all day. And all night, she is coughing . . ."

"Do you know who this fisherman is?" Maureen asked him gently. "Where he came from?"

Kalu shook his head. "His name is Mister Elliot. He talks English and his face is white."

"Where did you meet him?"

"Um, a town near the sea, in the fish market beside the dock where there are many boats. I tell him I work hard for him on the boat, cheap."

"And Aisha?"

"Aisha can help cook."

"But what about your parents? Your mother and father?"

"My father's gone long time now. Since I was small. And after the soldiers with guns come, they take everyone in my village, and my mother, she, she . . ." Here Kalu was overcome with emotion. He put his hands to his face and shook his head.

"It's all right, my little man." Maureen patted his shoulder. "You're safe here. Have more tea and biscuits. I'm making my famous beef and potato stew for our tea later." She left to stir the steaming pot on the stove.

Kalu sniffed a long sniff then wiped his eyes on the back of his hands.

"Your aunt, she is kind." He pulled my mother's pouch off his neck and gave it to me. "The bag with the watch. You keep now."

That's when I knew he finally trusted me.

The afternoon passed slowly for me. Clouds had gathered and it was raining hard. Kalu curled up on the sofa. He couldn't take his eyes away from the TV. He was mesmerized by the flickering picture.

I found the Selkie book on Maureen's shelves and a comfortable chair by the window where I could watch the rain lashing the water down at the dock. But I was restless. I peeked into my bedroom. Aisha was fast asleep, breathing regularly.

"Sleep is the best thing for that little mite," Maureen said. "Now I have some chores I must attend to in the lighthouse."

"Want help?"

Maureen raised her eyebrows at my offer. "Why, yes. Yes, that would be lovely. I'm sure the kids will be fine without us for a while."

We pulled on raincoats, and after telling Kalu where we were going, I followed her through the rain to the lighthouse. We checked that the connections on the new generator were okay, and I followed her up the spiral stairs to the lamp room. Hoisting an old metal oil can, Maureen dabbed oil onto the machinery that held the big lamp.

"If you want to give me a hand, the windows around the lamp can always be cleaned again. Amazing it is, that even the insides get so mucked up in just a day or two. It's the salt air. I have a fresh squirt bottle of vinegar and a new chamois I bought yesterday. Then you can use a bit of newspaper to give them a good polish."

I picked up the bottle and leather chamois and started on the windows. "Can you tell me more about my mother? What she was like?"

"Oh, your mother." Maureen smiled sadly. "Well, love, she was the best friend you could ever imagine. Lively and funny. So funny. But she could be fierce too. Once a bunch of girls at school were picking on a newcomer, calling her Fatso. When Lela heard that, she just ploughed into those bullies and told them if they ever teased the girl again, they'd feel the weight of her fist right in their faces."

I laughed. It was something I could imagine myself doing. "So what did the girls do?"

"They laughed at *her*. But you know, they never did tease the new girl again. Your mother was ferocious about coming to people's aid. Everyone's aid. Sometimes it could actually be embarrassing. She was always collecting for some project, like Save the Children. A bit like you with Kalu and Aisha. Wonder what their whole story is."

I shook my head. "It's a mystery all right. He told us about how they caught a ride with a fisherman in his boat, so that explains how they got to the island."

"Yes. I imagine the fisherman was worried if the kids were caught on his boat, he'd get into serious trouble harbouring illegal people. Maybe he even intended to come back and pick them up when it was safe, but probably not."

"So what are we going to do?"

"The first thing is to get Aisha better. Poor sweetie. Good thing you found her when you did. She may even have a touch of pneumonia."

"That's what I thought. But if anyone finds out she and Kalu are here, what will happen? Maybe they'll send them back to the very place they had to escape from. That would be friggin' terrible. We can't let that happen. Right?"

"Right." Maureen's lips turned up into a broad smile that crinkled her eyes. "You do so remind me of your mother."

"My mother. If it wasn't for me, she'd probably still be alive."

"Why ever do you say that?"

"Well." I shrugged. "She died when I was born." I swallowed hard at the sudden lump in my throat. "I was the cause of her death. I made her die." There. I'd admitted the terrible truth out loud. Now the whole world would come crashing down on my head.

"Oh, Spike." Maureen squeezed my shoulder. "It wasn't your fault your mother died. You should never think that. Not for an instant. Sometimes these things just happen."

"But she died. And, and I think my father always blamed . . ."

"Then he was an ignorant old fool. You know what? When I look at you, it's like seeing your mom looking out through your very eyes, so it is. She would have been so proud of you."

"Proud? Really? You really think so?"

"That I do, indeed." She grinned at me.

I didn't know what to say.

"You know, Spike. I can't tell you how lovely it is having you here on the island. And I hope you'll be staying on with me for a good long time."

I felt a gush of what? Happiness? Joy? Then why were my eyes damp? I wiped them on the back of my hand and bent to rub the lighthouse glass clean. That was the first time, except maybe that brief brush with the travelling musicians in Dublin, that I could remember anyone had ever said they liked having me around. It's true, I had some good friends at St. Bridgette's, but school could never be home.

Maybe I could stay here for a while after all.

There were worst places in the world than Last Chance Island.

Chapter 43

KALU

IT WAS A FEW months later. They were sitting around the big kitchen table, the three of them. Kalu was sitting between Aisha and the tall girl who liked to be called Spike. Although sometimes they called her Lil and she didn't seem to mind that at all, Kalu noticed.

Auntie Maureen was at the counter punching down dough for the bread she and Aisha were making.

They were doing "book work," as they did for a few hours every morning. Auntie insisted on it. Aisha's English was getting pretty good. Her accent was even more Irish than Auntie's. It helped that her two front teeth were growing in now.

Kalu heard the sound of a boat approaching the dock.

Auntie peered out the kitchen window. "Looks like Seamus," she said, wiping her hands on her apron. "Wonder what he has for us today. You kids want to go check? Tell him I'm putting the kettle on for tea."

Kalu followed Spike and Aisha who was the quickest to scamper away from the table. The three of them jogged down to the dock. It was a warm day with sunshine bouncing off the sea.

"Some mail. And a package, special delivery for you, young man," Seamus announced, as Kalu tied the water taxi to the iron ring on the landing float.

"For me?" Kalu couldn't believe it. He'd never in his life received mail from anyone.

"Open, open," Aisha said, hopping from one bare foot to the other.

"There's a package for you as well, young lady."

"Oooh," she said, hugging it.

"Let's take them up to the house before you open them," Spike said. "Maureen will want to see what's in them too. She's making a cup of tea for you, Seamus."

"Wouldn't say no to a cuppa." He followed the kids to the house carrying the rest of the mail.

"Auntie, Auntie!" Aisha called, as they all hurried inside. "Package come for Kalu. For me too."

"Oh my. They've arrived already, so they have."

Kalu put his package on the table. "You know about this package, Auntie?"

"It's a treat for your birthday. And one for Aisha too."

"Birthday?"

"I don't know when your birthdays are, but I thought it would be fun to celebrate today since it's the solstice, the first day of summer. So I made a special cake for you both. Now sit down, everyone."

Kalu helped Spike push their study books aside, and they all sat around the big kitchen table, even Seamus.

Auntie opened the cupboard beside the sink and brought out a cake covered with icing. "It's a pineapple cake. With coconut icing."

Kalu's mouth watered when he saw it. There were two candles on top.

"One candle for Kalu, and one for you, Aisha," Auntie said, carrying the cake to the table.

Seamus lit the candles. They sang the "Happy Birthday" song.

"Now before blowing out the candles," Spike told them, "you have to make a wish."

Kalu looked at Spike's smiling face, at Auntie and Seamus. Although he missed his brother and his mother, and all the other people in his village, he wished that he could stay here on this beautiful island with these kind people forever. And looking at Aisha, he thought that's what her wish was as well.

They both blew out the candles at the same time and everyone clapped and cheered. Even Aisha and Kalu.

Spike helped bring over the cups for tea and plates for the cake.

"Should we have cake first, or open the packages?" Auntie asked.

"Cake," Kalu said, eyeing the swirly icing sprinkled with coconut. In spite of three good meals a day, he could never pass up the chance to eat something so delicious looking.

"Package," Aisha sang out.

"OK, Aisha, you can open your special package."

Aisha did. Her eyes grew enormous when she saw what was inside. "Shoes! I never have shoes! Never, never!" She took out the shiny red leather sandals and held them up to her cheek.

"Try them on, love. I hope they fit."

Spike helped her do up the buckles and she sashayed around the table, her skinny hips swaying.

"Ha!" Kalu laughed. "Aisha is walking like she is a big lady from the town."

Aisha grinned at him as she gave Auntie a big hug. "Thank you, Auntie. Red shoes so beauty-ful."

"Now, what about you, Kalu? Will you still have cake first, or your package?"

"Cake," Kalu said again. "Please, Auntie."

Spike groaned. "We'll never get to see what's in his package."

"It's his choice," Auntie Maureen said as she passed around thick wedges of cake. Kalu finished his piece before Spike had hardly started hers. She groaned even louder when Auntie Maureen offered him a second slice, which he accepted with a grin.

Finally, he finished both pieces.

Auntie said, "You better open your package, Kalu, before Spike explodes with curiosity."

Kalu tore open the long narrow package, which revealed a black case. He opened the case, and when he saw what was inside, he gasped. "No!" he whispered. "I do not believe ..."

"What is it? What is it?" Spike asked.

Kalu reverently lifted his gift from the box. It caught the sunlight. "A flute," he said. "A beautiful, beautiful silver flute. Thank you, Auntie. Thank you."

"Try it out," she suggested. "See if it works."

"You blow here," Seamus pointed to a hole near one end of the flute.

Kalu stood up, moistened his lips and raised the flute. He blew into the hole Seamus had shown him. At first the only sound he could get out of it was a muffled sort of wheeze.

"Try arranging your fingers over the holes like so," Seamus said.

Kalu readjusted his fingers to fit over the holes. He blew gently. One note came out, and another, and another. He tried different finger combinations, different positions for his lips. Playing this flute was quite different from playing his old bamboo flute. After a few false starts, he was able to play a simple tune. And another. Then he tried a livelier one.

Aisha danced around the table wearing her new red sandals and Spike joined her twirling and spinning around the kitchen.

They all clapped after Kalu played the final flourish to his tune.

"That is the thank-you song," he said, bowing. "Thank you, Auntie, for the flute. And the delicious cake. And thank you for our home. For our family."

Aisha gave Auntie another hug. Auntie smiled, and Kalu saw her eyes were shiny as if she had tears in them. Happy tears.

"Thank you, Uncle, for bringing the gifts," he said to Seamus.

Seamus nodded. "As I've told you, the Isle of Last Chance is the Beginning Place ..."

Kalu glanced out the window at a couple of gulls flying past the lighthouse, the sun glinting off their outstretched wings.

"And Spike ..." he said.

"The name's Lil now," she announced.

"Thank you most, Lil." Kalu bumped her fist with his, as she'd taught him to do.

And he looked around his new home, at his new family.

A few days later, Lil was doing some research on the computer while the three of them were at the kitchen table doing their "book work."

"Look at this, Kal." She nudged his shoulder. "Says here they're starting a crowdfunding project to raise money to try to find some kids kidnapped from a school in Nigeria. That's where you and Aisha are from, right?"

Looking up from his math book, Kalu nodded. The picture on the computer screen was of several girls huddled together. He tried to search their faces to see if he recognized any classmates from his village school but the girls were hidden by black headscarves. His throat closed at the thought of what terrible things would be happening to his friends.

"So do you think you'll ever go back home one day?" Lil asked him.

"Home?" He cleared his throat. "This is my home now. Our family, Aisha and me. With Auntie and you. On Last Chance Island."

"But don't you long for Africa sometimes?"

"In Africa there is no one left for us. But maybe one day. Maybe I could go back there to teach in the villages. Maybe a music teacher? I could show the kids how to make music with the bamboo flute like my teacher showed me."

He picked up his new flute that was always close by and played a trill that soon became a medley of tunes that made Lil think of the warmth and sunshine of the place he and Aisha had left. There was also a sadness that ran through his music. A sadness and longing for his homeland in Africa as it used to be.

"Hey, dude," Lil said, when his music came to an end. "Maybe in a few years we can all make a trip there, see what there is to see. Maybe even help out in some way. Who knows?"

"Who knows," he said.

Epilogue

SPIKE

IT TOOK MAUREEN and me months of writing pleas and memos to the Irish refugee board. It all led to visits from several authorities. Eventually, after hearing Kalu's story about his village and contacting the Nigerian government, it was agreed that he and Aisha could stay on with Maureen on Last Chance Island.

I stayed as well. There's so much to do here with helping Maureen look after the light, exploring every corner of the island, taking the kids out fishing near the dock, I even sort of forgot about Kieran and his troupe of musicians. Funny. That night I met them in Dublin feels as if it belongs to a whole other life. And I feel like a whole different person.

Maureen's still quite strict about school. We have to do "book work" every day, mostly using distance education. Aisha loves helping Maureen in the kitchen. Maureen says she's a born cook. Kalu is learning a lot about music. Especially after Maureen bought him that cool flute. His playing and composing new tunes are really something else. Every single day he amazes us. Especially at sunset when he goes out to play to the sun as it sinks into the horizon.

Because of our help keeping the lighthouse going, the threat of automating the light has been dropped. The Commissioners of Irish Lights agreed that Last Chance Light should remain "manned" for the foreseeable future. With Seamus's assistance, we're even building an extension to the house, a sort of kids' wing so we'll each have our own rooms. Then no one will have to sleep in the sitting room anymore.

And my father's estate? We heard from his lawyer, Farley Wilson that, in his will, my father has left me enough funds to go to university when I graduate from high school — if I want. There's also a substantial monthly allowance that Farley's started sending Maureen for my board. So that should help the situation here on Last Chance with the extra mouths to feed.

Some people might think we're a weird bunch of people living together. But to me, it feels like family.

And Last Chance Island feels like home.

ABOUT THE AUTHOR

Norma Charles is the author of nineteen books for children, including recent Gold Medal Moonbeam Award winner *Run Marco, Run*. She was a teacher-librarian for many years in Vancouver, where she lives with her family — except when she can get away to Hardy Island off the Sunshine Coast. She and her partner Brian have a most delightful summer place there, which is a little like Last Chance Island without the lighthouse. Visit her website at www.normacharles.ca.

MARQUIS

Québec, Canada

RECYCLED
Paper made from
recycled material
FSC® C103567